REMEMBRANCE DAY

Remembrance Day

THITEEN ATTEMPTS
IN PROSE TO ADOPT AN
ATTITUDE OF RESPECT

GERHARD ZWERENZ

*Translated from the German by
Eric Mosbacher*

HUTCHINSON OF LONDON

HUTCHINSON & CO (*Publishers*) LTD
178-202 Great Portland Street, London, W1

London Melbourne Sydney
Auckland Bombay Toronto
Johannesburg New York

First published in Germany
by Scherz under the title
of HELDENGEDENKTAG
First published in Great Britain 1966

English translation
© Hutchinson & Co (Publishers) Ltd
and E. P. Dutton & Co Inc, New York, 1966

This book has been set in Plantin
printed in Great Britain on Antique Wove paper
by Cheltenham Press Ltd, Cheltenham, and
bound by Wm. Brendon & Son Ltd,
Tiptree, Essex

*I think of my ego
through a
magnifying glass*

E. T. A. HOFFMAN

Instead of a Foreword
BLACK CALENDAR HOPE
for E.B.

1

Hope, said the preacher,
I bid you hope,
You can hope,
I bid you hope.

Hope, I say,
A philosopher wrote a hundred books about it
and you have read them all.
But I say
hope is a black calendar.

Tear off sheet after sheet.
Hope goes with them all.
And I say it is nothing but
a black calendar.

2

So I stand and pull off sheet
after sheet, holding my hand to my face and thinking
now a lucky white sheet is coming.

3

Mighty is hope
we persevere in its shadow
on its banks we await our ship
in its honour we build towers and domes
because of it we dream
we pray for it to smile.
Hope, mighty sister.

Mighty is hope
that the day shall endure
that no silence shall stifle its voice
that no slayer shall stab it to the heart
that no water shall hinder its steps
that no height shall remain unattainable.
Hope, mighty sister.

4

You shine in graves
in women's wombs
in the heads of sleepers
in the heads of the wise

you burgeon from the trees
you are grass in the sunlight
and the sunlight over the grass
you are hunger and thirst.

5

Mighty is hope
The Temple of Jerusalem
fearful avenger
sickle of the mighty
sickle of the helpless
spring of those who are autumn
fearful avenger.
Hope, mighty mistress.

6

In your body the sexes
in your sleep our dreams
in your sight our day
in your timelessness our time

You are our vulnerability
you are our holy error
you are the remnant of our reality
our poem.

Mighty is hope
man climbs mountains
mighty is hope
man descends into the seas
mighty is hope.

In his books man discovers
himself; but you are the discoverer
of discovery.
Hope, mighty mother.

7

Cronus, son of Uranus and Gaea,
unmanned and deposed his father,
assumed his throne and married
Rhea, his sister.

Cronus, son of Uranus and Gaea,
for whom a similar end was prophesied,
devoured his children
so that he should not be devoured himself.

Cronus, son of Uranus and Gaea,
devoured immediately after their birth
Hestia, Demeter, Hera, Pluto, Poseidon
like stones wrapped in swaddling clothes.

Cronus, son of Uranus and Gaea,
was outwitted by Rhea, his wife,
who spared her youngest, Zeus,
feeding his father a stone instead.

Cronus, son of Uranus and Gaea,
when his son Zeus grew to manhood
was flung by him down into
Tartarus. Men, give your monsters
stones to eat.

Hope, mighty mother!

THE MOLE

HE KNELT down on the hard ground, not to pray, but to dig. Each time he drove his spade into it, it sent a stab of pain up into his body, from his ankles into his stout boots, from his knees up into his belly, chest and arms, and right into his grimy, over-grown finger-nails.

He was one of those who had learnt to adapt themselves to the requirements of the day. He was digging a hole. The earth was hard, but he was driving a hole into it. The night was dark, the air damp, and the earth dry and so hard that it might have been frozen. Clouds advanced through an invisible sky, which you could feel though you could not see, and under it there was the relentless energy of a man driving his spade into the ground, and every now and then, in this direction or in that, a shot leapt forth and faded into the spaces of the night.

The hole was not yet eighteen inches deep. The pain mounted to his head, from where it pressed out against the arch of his brow and crept into his ears, making them hum and buzz – who could be thinking about him? – and popped out of his eyes, out into the night and down into the hard earth that reared and crumbled under the cutting and scraping of the spade.

He was not just digging a hole. The earth he dug out of it he used to form a parapet to protect his head and shoulders. When the sun rose in a few hours time it would shine on a mound concealed with greenery and brushwood, a camouflaged position, behind which there lurked the invisible eyes of a sniper.

He sweated and panted, and the pain faded away.

Sweat poured down under his helmet, crept round his eyes and from the bridge of his nose down on to his cheeks and mingled with his silent or muttered imprecations.

He cursed this hard earth, and thought longingly of soft, white sand, for he came from a place where earth and sea met, and the soft, white sand was as alluring as a bed, an embrace. Rage rose within him, and he cursed aloud. Dig, he ordered himself, dig, damn you, dig deeper, dig yourself in properly, dig.

Dig, you bastard.

Sullenly he dug deeper. He must have got eighteen inches deep. He rose to his feet, scrambled out of the hole, jumped back into it with his feet together, and landed with a dull thud. Yes, eighteen inches, he said to himself, only to be overcome with a sense of frustration. What was the good of eighteen inches? That didn't provide much safety.

He went on digging. He had dug his first hole, the first of his innumerable holes, when he was ten, and that had been for no warlike purpose. He and several other boys had wanted to dig themselves a house in the earth for fun, but before they finished the peasant to whom the bit of woodland belonged had turned up and given them a good hiding. The memory cheered him somewhat, and he nearly smiled. He had been good at digging even when he was a boy, and those few strokes that the peasant had given them hadn't done them any harm. It hadn't done him any harm either. He was good at digging.

He had to admit that he wasn't very strong; he didn't take easily to digging. Sometimes he wished he had been a navvy, used to heavy labour from his youth, with great rippling muscles on his chest and legs. That would have made things much easier. Or he should have been a blacksmith with biceps as big as a fist.

He had dug his first military foxhole about two years ago. Was it really only about two years ago? That wasn't long. Surprising. Then he had been a raw, young, unlicked cub, stupid, curious, and simple. They had just arrived at the front, a platoon of green, anonymous young soldiers, and they dug themselves in on a hillside. When firing broke out, they pressed their faces into the ground and the shots whistled over their heads. They were a reserve platoon in a reserve position, in dead ground; the hill was sheltered from the enemy, from the wind, and from shell-fire. On that first day they all lay in their holes and slept. In the evening they crept out, stretched their limbs, and went and got a meal; the field kitchen came up in the shelter of darkness. Then they went back to their holes to go to sleep again. Sleep? This time he had not been able to go to sleep. More out of boredom than anything else, he had picked up his spade and gone on digging.

Then he went fast asleep for the rest of the night, and slept through most of the next day, too, and wrote only a brief letter home. That night the field kitchen produced bacon and peas, and he dug his hole still deeper. It was now really very deep indeed, and on the next evening they ragged him about it. Had he got the wind up? Did he want to tunnel his way through to the other side and desert? Or had he found coal at least?

On the afternoon of the third day he went off on his own. It was perfectly simple. He a coward? What next? He picked up his rifle, clambered out of the hole, and tramped up the slope from the top of which the enemy position was visible. A lance-corporal saw him go, but lay down in his hole and went off to sleep again. All the others were asleep, too. What else was there to do when one was in reserve?

He made his way towards the top. If anyone had stopped him and asked him what he was doing, he would not have known what to say. He crept through some prickly bushes on which shiny blackberries as big as plums were hanging, with bees buzzing busily all round them, stumbled into a half finished or half collapsed trench, caught his foot on a putrifying body, and kicked a mess-tin – who had last used it? At last he reached the top. The earth fell away below him like a bowl, and the plain, the enemy plain, stretched out in front of him.

He flung himself down, took cover, and put his eye to the telescopic sight of his rifle.

He watched the enemy like a tiger watching its prey. He watched the way it moved, visualising the best way of attack and its possible counter-moves, he estimated the range and grew cold with resolution. Meanwhile the enemy went comfortably on his way, as if he were strolling round the corner to buy a packet of cigarettes. He wore narrow, stove-pipe trousers, the tail of his jacket fluttered in the wind, and his hands were deep in his trouser-pockets, almost up to the elbows. He was strolling along as if totally unaware that he was an enemy.

The thin, round barrel followed him to the left with a uniform, almost sympathetic, movement reliably composed of steel and wood and human hands that could hold bread and butter and pen-holders and rifles.

Meanwhile the enemy was making his way in leisurely fashion in the direction of some bushes. He still had perhaps twenty yards to go; then he would disappear behind them, escape with his life, never even suspect what he had been so close to. In a moment the bushes would enclose him. (What did he want to do behind them? Smoke a cigarette? Relieve himself? Or was he, too, in reserve and bored to death?)

Strolling along with his hands in his pockets, he was unaware of a thread-like cross that followed and clung to him and did not let him go until a cold grey eye had him and the cross in line and the pupil suddenly narrowed and a finger moved, too, as if a thread running from eye to finger had been pulled simultaneously. The enemy fell to the ground with a gash in his throat.

That was about two years ago, he said to himself, driving his spade into the ground. The hole was now about two feet deep, and in the morning it would be a deep, narrow, safe slit. The first hole he had dug had been deep and narrow, too. At first he had dug deeper out of sheer boredom, and when he came back from the hill-top he had gone on digging, with the sight of the enemy still in his eyes, the enemy with a gash in his throat. But during the night an artillery barrage was laid down and went on for two hours, and then it died away and ceased at 3.10 a.m. precisely. For two hours it raised long rows of fiery fountains of earth, mushrooms that sprang suddenly out of the earth and burnt themselves out in a moment, sending glowing fragments of metal and bits of stone all round that hissed and died and landed with dull thuds, tearing bodies to pieces. That morning there was no proper dawn, for a black, toxic cloud lay over the country and held back the light. There were no casualties in the reserve platoon, which lay disregarded in the shelter of the hill, in dead ground, in which men could live; not a single shell landed in the field where it lay. The men looked over the parapets of their slit trenches through inflamed, watering eyes, small-arms fire announced an enemy attack, and now a human form appeared and stopped, and announced itself as the battalion runner. 'I've got to go forward, and someone's got to come with me,' he said. The men looked out of their holes, looking as if they had been decapitated. 'Come on, one of you has got to come with me.' The runner went up to one of the holes. It was deep, quite unnecessarily deep, and at the bottom of it a human form was crouching. The toe of the runner's boot caused bits of earth to drop down inside it. 'Come on, you, you're coming with me,' he said.

He crept out and went. The day before he had

conducted a private war of his own, but now he was given an order and obeyed.

On their way back they had nearly reached the reserve platoon's position again when all hell broke loose, and they flung themselves to the ground. Shells furrowed the air overhead burning hot, exploded drily quite close to them, and the blast burnt their skin. After it stopped the silence was painful, disturbed as it was by a crescendo of faint groans.

Then he found himself in the field where the reserve platoon had lain, and all round him the broken earth was steaming, and lumps of flesh lay about, most of it motionless but some still quivering and calling for help. Now the earth could drink its fill. But he stopped in front of one of the holes, which was narrow and very deep, and he looked down and saw a spade lying at the bottom. He jumped down, picked it up, clambered out again, and stood there. The only thing that had survived the destruction was his hole. *His* hole? The field had been cut to pieces, the safe, protective trenches had been destroyed and buried, and a lot were smeared as if with red paint, but he was still alive.

He was safe, he had been spared, he was still alive. It could, of course, be explained quite simply. Later he thought about it a lot. First there had been the barrage, and then the attack. The artillery had changed position, and the reserve platoon now lay in its field of fire.

That was the natural, simple, obvious explanation. But it was a stupid and false explanation. Why had it been he who had gone with the runner?

Why he rather than any of the others? The others had stayed in their place of safety, their place of assumed safety, and had died, and he had gone with the runner and survived. Had he not been given a sign? For even if he had not gone, even if the runner had not appeared on the scene and he had stayed in his hole like the rest he would have survived. His spade, his bit of tarpaulin, his haversack, his water-bottle, all lay tidy and undamaged at the bottom of it. Was it not a sign? Why should it not be a sign? A feeling came over him gently bidding him to kneel and say thanks for having been chosen to survive. But he did not yield to it, for he was swept up in the wave of troops that came surging back from the front line and carried him along and spilled him forth, and he went with them, panting and yet glad, and for the next two years he had gone with them through this never-ending enemy country, marching and firing and advancing and retreating and digging himself in. He carefully counted every hole he dug, and he always kept on digging until it was as deep and narrow as the first. It was subject to this condition that he had been chosen, and he observed it faithfully. He was brave, he was a sniper, and afterwards he snuggled into his deep trench.

As he lay in his thirty-third hole he received a warning. As usual, it was deep, and he lay at the bottom. He had dug all his thirty-three holes narrow and deep like this. It was raining, and he shivered with cold. His platoon lay in a gently sloping field, the grass was rotting, the soil was clay and smelt of decay. Tiny streams snaked their way through it, with innumerable ramifications, and new ones formed daily. He had stretched his ground-sheet over his hole and loaded it with stones to keep it straight, and, though the earth on which he lay was not dry, at least he was protected from the rain. Just when he was getting up an ear-splitting crash knocked him back again, and the blast seemed to stamp him into the ground. When he recovered himself and looked up he saw a small tear in the ground-sheet over his head through which he could see a patch of sky heavy with rain. It was obvious what had happened. A grenade-thrower had scored a direct hit on his hole, and he had been saved from death by his ground-sheet, which had set off the sensitive percussion fuze and sent the charge upwards.

After this he always dug a lateral extension to his trench, so that in the event of another direct hit he would still be safe. Not satisfied with digging deep, he also dug a narrow passage to one side leading to an almost completely enclosed little dug-out in which he could dwell in dark security, and he kept to this procedure from his thirty-third hole to his eighty-sixth. This caused him to be known as the mole, but he was allowed to go his own way, because there were forty-four notches on the shaft of his rifle, and he had become a legendary figure. He was known at regiment and division, and had been mentioned in the official *communiqué*. He was an outstanding sniper. He hit his mark and then crept deep into the earth. He had become a hero and, though everyone else had to share his slit trench with a companion, he was allowed to remain alone.

Light began timidly advancing from the east over the torn up earth, and on both sides of the front the weapons awoke. The first shots cleft through the air and either missed or found their target. His hole was now six feet deep, and he could stand upright in it and still be safe, for he was invisible, and no rifle or machine-gun bullet could reach him. Now he must dig to one side, so that shells and bombs and splinters could not reach him either. He knelt and picked up his spade to dig the lateral passage, but then stopped. No, it won't do, he said to himself, for soon he would be overtaken by daylight, when the front would awaken completely and there must be no more movement, for a spadeful of earth flung out into the open might betray his hiding-place. Hurriedly and strenuously he set about digging his hole eighteen inches deeper, eighteen inches deeper than was really necessary. The earth was noticeably soft on one side, and he finished the job quickly, and then crept outside and covered the earth he had flung out with grass and brushwood. Then he jumped back into the hole and began digging his lateral passage eighteen inches above the bottom. The earth that he now dug out – and once more he was surprised at how soft it was – he could simply leave at the bottom of the trench, for he had dug it extra deep for this purpose and there was no need to shovel any of it outside.

He made his lateral passage just wide enough to

crawl through. After digging to three feet, he
decided he had gone far enough in that direction,
and then he began digging his real, secure dug-out,
leading off it at an angle of ninety degrees. If a
bomb or shell exploded in his trench now, splinters would fly into the lateral passage and bury
themselves in the earth, but they could not turn
an angle of ninety degrees into the dug-out.

Outside it was now broad daylight. He lay in the
lateral passage, holding his spade in both hands,
and raged at his tiredness. He attacked the earth as
if it were an enemy, drove the spade into it, boring
and biting into it and turning it. He went on digging,
and earth collapsed over his head and fell on his
helmet and shoulders and covered his back and
arms, but he kept digging away, and when he was
nearly buried in collapsing earth he pushed it back
behind him with arms and legs, chest and belly and
face, so that it fell out into the passage and the slit
trench, where it covered the ground like black
snow. He was breathing heavily. There was a smell
of damp and darkness, clay and fields and gardens,
and he liked this kind of smell, because it reminded
him of the smell of water and sand at home.

Only later did he notice the sharp smell of
decomposition. When he did notice it, he hesitated
for a moment. Decomposition at this depth? But he
was tired, and needed all his strength to finish the
job. He mustn't weaken now. By this time he was
deep in the earth, surrounded by darkness; only a
faint, broken gleam of light reached him over his
shoulders, a distant reflection of the outside world
from which he wished to protect himself. Lumps of

earth fell on his helmet and his behind, but he took no notice, he knew what he was doing, he knew all these noises, he had experienced earth in all its forms, and it had no more secrets or surprises for him.

Suddenly he felt exhausted and had to stop for a breather. He crept back a little way, fumbled in his pocket for his lighter, put a cigarette between his lips, lit it, and inhaled deeply. But smoking did not do him any good. Eighty-six holes in many countries had taken their toll, and for weeks past he had marched, dug, fired his rifle and eaten little.

He was lying there in a strange state of irresolution, previously unknown to him, when things started up outside. They reached his ear as if from a great distance. Artillery began systematically shelling the area, and there were some bursts quite close, he could feel the blast, and this brought him back to himself with a start. He swore, and told himself that he would get himself killed all because he was lying here idly when he had only such a short way to go to safety. Had he dug eighty-six holes only to be caught here like a rat in a trap? What had all that effort, and all those notches on the shaft of his rifle, and all that straining and sweating been for? He had been chosen on condition that he played his part. Events had taught him that he must fight and then dig himself safely in. He was a marksman and a mole, he must kill and then ensure his own safety, and that was his duty. If he failed in it, the spell would be broken. He must be strong and crafty, cold and cunning. He blazed up. No, they weren't going to get him. There

flashed into his mind the hole he had dug in ten
seconds flat. He had been at home on leave, had
gone down to the shore, flung himself down on the
sand, crept into it. A squad of young recruits had
come marching along to practise trench-digging in
the broom-covered sandy expanse behind the
beach, and he had got up and gone over to them,
and got into conversation with the n.c.o. in charge.
He said he could disappear into the ground in ten
seconds. Ten seconds? The n.c.o. had laughed.
Very well, would he like to have a bet on it then?
The n.c.o. had agreed, and then he had astonished
them all, not merely the recruits and the n.c.o., but
the whole training staff, including the officers, who
had come crowding round to watch him vanishing
into the ground in ten seconds, using spade and
elbows, knees and feet, even his chin. It had been
child's play, of course, because the soil was light,
you only had to understand it, as soon as you had
kicked away the surface growth you came to sand,
but they had gaped at him as if he were a man from
another planet. Ten seconds flat, just imagine it!
They had tried to imitate him, but the nearest they
got was thirty seconds, just three times as long as he.

The secret was energy and using your wits. That
was the secret of survival, and he knew what he
wanted, and what he wanted was to survive. Yes,
and he would survive. With a maximum of pre-
caution and a maximum of heroism. With the
notches on his rifle-butt and his mole-holes. He
spat contemptuously and burrowed once more into
the earth. Angrily he withdrew his arms and then
plunged them in again. When he struck his spade

into the dark wall he felt a stab of pain in his belly, but he went for the wall as if he were throttling an enemy, boring into it, gritting his teeth and straining the lungs inside him that beat against his ribs. As he worked forward it got easier and easier, the earth crumbled away in front of him and rained down on top of him, embracing and concealing him. This strange softness of the earth began to bewilder and oppress him and, though he went on digging, he could not help thinking about it. At first it had been as hard as iron, but here it was loose and soft. This was unprecedented in all his experience, and he had plenty. Or was he perhaps not the first to dig in this place? Had there not been fighting here in the previous war? Was he digging himself into a First World War position? Hell, what did it matter? All he cared about was his own safety. Suddenly something came over him, his strength failed as if his blood were ebbing away, and he lay still in the earthy darkness, an exhausted body drained of its strength, sweaty and cold and bent and covered in grime.

The first thing he noticed when he came to was the sharp smell. This, so deep underground, was also a totally new phenomenon to him. A violent feeling of nausea made him move. He raised his head, but his helmet was inhumanly heavy. He groped for his spade and found it, and felt with alarming clarity the weight on the back of his legs. He lay on his belly and tried to turn round, but he was stuck. I'm half dazed, he said to himself, feeling surprised at the clarity of the thought.

He felt as if he were asleep but could think clearly
in spite of it. Once more something rose inside him,
his stomach mounted up into his throat, pressed
violently into it, and he had a violent feeling
of nausea, and through the sharp smell of decay he
could distinguish the sweet, sickly smell of recent
decomposition. Desperately he turned to struggle
free from the trap. He pulled his legs out of the
muck, pulling off his boots in the process, and
found himself lying on his back, still with a firm
grip on the shaft of his spade, and then realised
for the first time that he could not see even a
gleam of daylight. He was plunged in darkness,
night had fallen for him. Desperately he attacked
the darkness, drove his spade into it, fought to
drive it away from him, to strangle it, kill it, but
his strength failed. His hands refused to obey him,
he trembled and quivered and panted and wanted
to cry out, and when he came to again he was
half buried and had lost all sense of direction, of
where he lay, of where the passage was, or the
trench, or the front, or the enemy. The earth
tasted sweet, he was going to suffocate, he was
suffocating, he kicked out behind him with his bare
feet, which met nothing but soft slipperiness. That
brought him to his senses. I must get out of this, he
said to himself in sudden calm. I mustn't lose my
nerve. He fumbled in his trouser-pocket, found
his lighter, and lit it. The tired, flickering flame
cast a feeble light and then went out. I'm still lying
in the direction I was in before, he said to himself, I
must turn and work back to the lateral passage.
Calmly he scraped away at the wall and forced him-

self round. Then the stifling, sickly sweetness got the better of him and he vomited, and all the time the only thought in his mind was that he must get out of this.

In the brief glow cast by his lighter he saw as in a picture what he had been overcome by, the naked bodies emerging from the earth into which they had been flung higgledy-piggledy.

He had dug himself under a mass grave. But all he cared about was safety, and he was a crafty old soldier who did not give in so easily. He groped behind him. The flame had gone out. He brought up blood and fear, but did not give in, with his energy and his sharp eyes and his patent holes he had safely come through everything so far, and he had no intention of throwing in the sponge now. He groped about and found the spade and grasped it, and prepared to assault the black wall and force his way through it. He stared at it and, though it was white and red, did not see it as it was, because he wanted it to be black, because it was easier to attack that way. He was an experienced, self-disciplined soldier, and he summoned up his strength, the strength of all his muscles, and cleared his throat to be able to breathe more freely and let the saliva flow – you should avoid letting your throat get dry. Was it fear that filled him? Yes, the fear that he had carried about with him always and every day, like the pack on his back or the heart in his breast. He had changed its name, called cowardice courage, insensitivity keenness, weakness energy. Fear? He had fled from death deep into the earth, escaped it at the price of the eighty-six

holes that he had dug and then left again, and the
forty-four more holes that had had to be dug for
the victims of his marksmanship. To emancipate
himself from fear he had trained his eye and killed
forty-four enemies. Forty-four, a strange, round
number. Fear? He had killed for the sake of escape
and survival, because he wanted to remain alive.
He had called his fear pride, had trusted his spade
and the hands that used it, and the small index
finger of his right hand that pulled the trigger. He
had thought it all out carefully. For two years of
the war he had lived according to a fixed plan, and
for two years he had succeeded in remaining alive.
In the army he had become a legendary figure. At
home schoolchildren knew his name, and the
enemy knew it, too, and whispered it. An aura of
fear and hate surrounded it, it had become a symbol
of valour and heroism. He would assault this wall
like a jackal falling on its prey, if need be, like a
hyena, he would . . . but he managed only to
struggle up on his knees, and his back hit the earth,
and he sank back again on his knees and forward
on to his hands, kneeling before the wall, the human wall, and his weakness drew his helmeted head
forward on to the earth, as if he were making an act
of obeisance, paying homage to the dead, perform-
ing an act of justice at last while his own life ebbed
away. Once more his strength returned. Was he
not as innocent as they? Had he had any more
choice than they? Had he not been shown the way
to get the better of the earth by entrusting himself
to it, incorporating himself in it? Had he not been
given a sign to live like this? Had he not right on

his side, the right to kill to avoid being killed himself? The dead who lay in front of him had not been killed by him. He had been a soldier, a brave soldier, perhaps the bravest in the army, in the whole war. The bravest and the cleverest.

A last spark of oxygen out of the earth made his lungs burn, and a faint gleam came into his eyes, like the reflection from a distant candle. He opened his mouth to speak, to mutter something, to pray. He spat into the dark earth that already enclosed his lips. He raised his head, felt the smooth, sweaty, worn wood of the shaft of his spade, and was still determined to work himself free. He flung himself forward, but not far enough, and the spade went sideways into the earth, scattering lumps of it over the dead bodies. Hope still blazed in him, furious hope of survival and escape. He worked on, got up on his knees, drove his spade into the earth, vomited green foam, subsided and forced himself up again, bit his tongue and lips, and saw and felt no more earth, blood and tears, the sense of fear and suffocation vanished, and he began to forget, first his name and then his calling, his country, his school, his father and mother, and last of all the dead around him and all that had happened. He went on digging and forgot his wishes and hopes, his dreams and fears, the war and the age in which he lived, and he dug through the dark earth, a lost, forgotten animal, and when death came it found him kneeling as senselessly as he had lived.

THE MONOGRAM

I WAS ordered to go to C. in the cause of justice. There I was to arrest a man and bring him back.

The order was given me by Schröter, my superior in the Department of Investigation into Counter-Revolutionary Crime.

'Very good, I'll leave straight away,' I said.

I took my shoes from in front of the stove, removed the crumpled paper I had stuffed into them to prevent them from losing their shape, and got into difficulties with the knotted laces. Schröter watched me attentively. I cut the knots with my pocket-knife, threaded the shortened laces, and tied them as best I could.

'Aren't you surprised at my sending you there?' asked Schröter.

'Why should I be?' I replied. 'Just because I come from the place?'

I walked round the desk and opened the drawer where my lunch was. A slice of bread and a salted herring. I had eaten the sausage first thing that morning when I got to the office. I bit the herring's head off, opened the window and spat it out. When the telephone rang, I answered. A peevish voice announced that the car was ready. Schröter was still watching me attentively. At the door I stumbled, and he gripped my arm.

'You'll bring him back, won't you? I can rely on you absolutely, can't I?'

I didn't answer, but went down to the yard where the car was waiting. It was the beginning of March, 1948, and a belated winter storm was rumbling. Stanek, the driver, took the road through Luckenwalde where we turned right and joined the *Autobahn* on the other side of Nossen. We had nearly two hundred miles to go, and it took us about ten hours. In the morning I saw the ruins of Chemnitz over towards the south. We drove on. Between Glauchau and Meerane we left the *Autobahn* and took the main road.

And so we got to C. The streets were deserted. Stanek looked at me distastefully, as if to say this was a rum sort of neighbourhood.

'To me it's home, and I like it,' I said.

Stanek drove to the New Market, stopped, pulled his coat over his face, dropped off to sleep and started snoring. I wandered about the town, went into St. Lawrence's, and had a look at the cemetery, the mortuary and the school. By midday I had had enough of it and walked up the steep street to the house on the Gablenzer Berg, where the two rooms were crammed full of beds, luggage, and pale, heavily breathing children. I had walked into the bedroom. The narrow yard below was unchanged. Only the pigeons were missing, they had long since been killed and eaten.

The occupants, German refugees from Hungary, whispered to each other. The children's eyes gleamed velvet. When I walked out the fear behind me turned to laughter. I refrained from explaining that it was my native place they were living in. My native place, that consisted of two rooms. With a big garden, that consisted of the round earthenware pots in which my mother grew flowers on the windowsill.

I walked downstairs, whistling, and stopped in

front of the old cellar door, where I bent down to
look at the monogram I had carved with my knife
when I was a boy. I touched the letters, and felt
completely at home, right down to my finger-
tips.

The storm was over, and the day was cold and
raw. Stanek emerged from under his coat. A few
thin, pale men and women were standing round the
car. You spend years in foreign countries, you kill
and are hunted yourself, you escape yet again, and
finally you end up where you began.

In the brickyard the car jolted over the cobbles
and stopped. The tall chimney disappeared into a
thin white cloud. A door beside the furnace steps
opened, clouds of dust rose, and a one-legged man
on crutches hobbled towards us.

'Hallo, Bruno,' I said.

He flushed scarlet, exclaimed, burst out laughing
and then stopped, and his pupils narrowed.

'Are you staying here?' he asked.

'Yes.'

'Have you got a big car like that, and a driver,
too?'

'Yes.'

The leafless birch-trees stayed motionless, and
huge spiders' webs gleamed in the warm eaves.
Bruno took an axe, chopped up an old shelf, and
put the rotten wood in the stove and made a fire.
The three of us sat there and listened to it crackling.

Some dogs howled hungrily outside.

When I awoke next morning Bruno was standing

by my bedside. In a voice hoarse with bitterness, he said:

'Now you're one of them, and you've come to fetch me, haven't you?'

'Go into the kitchen and wait for me,' I replied, and after he had turned his back I added: 'The proletariat has assumed power, and the proletariat is a just class, the only just class on earth.'

He hopped out, without his crutches. I got out of bed, pulled on my shirt and trousers, jacket and overcoat, picked up my pistol and charged it, and went into the kitchen. Bruno was leaning against the window. The storm was still raging and the sky was right outside the window-panes, a disc of frozen milk, and pale, white cold drove in from the Erzgebirge. I helped Bruno into his ragged overcoat, and he picked up his crutches. Stanek appeared, and we went outside.

'What have you got against me?' Bruno shouted.

'How do I know?' I said. 'Perhaps you killed some Russians,' I added indifferently.

'Yes, during the war,' Bruno shouted. 'I was in the army and killed Russians, and Russians killed us.'

He leant on one of his crutches, adroitly held the other between his elbow and his body, and with his free hand took himself by the throat.

Stanek was waiting by the car with the door open. The gale blew sand and stones on to the worn leather seats.

'And what about you?' Bruno shouted at me. 'Have you never killed anyone? Never? Are you sure?'

I drew my pistol.

'Get in,' I shouted. 'Get in, will you?' He got in, and I sat beside him.

'There's something I don't understand,' he said as we drove off. 'Major Tretiakov released me, and who's arresting me now?'

'There's also something I don't understand,' I said. 'Why did you stay here in the brickworks?'

'As if I had anywhere else to go. Tell me where I could go, just tell me. Get away on one leg? Just try it yourself, you won't get very far if you're a cripple, you take it from me. And as for going over to the Americans, they're waiting for me.'

'I see,' I said. 'And what was all that with Major Tretiakov, that was his name, wasn't it?'

'He's the chief at the NKWD headquarters at Chemnitz. I'm at his disposal.'

'Well, now you're at the disposal of Berlin headquarters,' I said. 'But you have my word of honour that nothing will happen to you.'

He began mumbling defiantly to himself. Later we played vingt et un, and when he dropped off to sleep I slipped the handcuffs on him. He awoke, stared silently at his wrists, and closed his eyes again.

We were somewhere in the neighbourhood of Chemnitz when he spoke again.

'That must be a hard job you've got, having to take your own friend to the gallows,' he said.

'That's quite true,' I replied. 'But you're talking to a representative of the working class. The revolution is a hard mother, but she is also a just one. Its individual soldiers may perish, anguish may break their hearts, but the revolution is immortal and its army is innumerable. The time is ripe. A war was lost, but a revolution won.'

'You've turned into a Siberian wolf,' Bruno said in impotent rage and fear, bringing his face close to mine.

'Our children will have a good life,' I said, 'and our grandchildren will not know what the liberation of a class means. There will be only one single class on earth – the liberated working class, a fine, proud and upright race.'

We drove on in silence.

'But, whatever you do, you've got a conscience, in your place I should act differently,' Bruno whispered.

'I am acting differently, Bruno,' I whispered back, and I took the key and unlocked his handcuffs.

We drove on through snow and slush. Every now and then the tyres slipped. Wind tore through the car.

'Stop,' I called out.

Stanek drew in to the side of the road.

'Get out, Bruno,' I shouted excitedly. 'Get out, quick.' He stopped on his crutches by the open door, gazing at the pistol in my hands. 'Clear off, you fool,' I shouted again, pointing the pistol at Stanek's back, and Bruno's deathly pale face vanished. He hopped off quickly through the falling snow. He staggered and fell and struggled up again, and then disappeared from sight.

When I reported to Schröter his eyes reddened

with anger. Disappointment cast a shadow over his
open face, he banged the desk with his fist, the
blood shot to his cheeks and brow, his bald patch
darkened, and he called me a traitor, a damned
traitor. He was an angry father to me.

'But you can't take a friend to the gallows,' I
said.

He took a deep breath and was going to answer,
but his features hardened, he coughed and choked
and then started spitting and spluttering, and I
noticed that he was spitting blood.

I felt a great liking for him again. He panted and
struggled for air, and then he sent for a policeman,
and they locked me up for a week in a cell in the
basement. Then on a Sunday night they sent for
me, and Schröter ordered me to go to a small town
on the zonal border to bring back Bruno. He had
escaped to the west, I was told, but the Americans
had picked him up and sent him back.

Bringing Bruno back again to Berlin was my last
job. Three years later they pushed him off a chair
in the vaulted basement of the Waldheim prison,
causing the clothes-line round his neck to tighten
and put an end to his life. But by that time I had
been out of it for three years. I admired Schröter.
When I brought Bruno into the room I noticed
how he was trembling with exhaustion, with the
pitiless midday light on his features. The Americans had sent Bruno back without his crutches,
heaven knows what had become of them, but he
would not have much use for them in future; in his
remaining span of life there would not be much
chance of movement.

'That was my last job. I'm going home,' I said to Schröter.

He came close up to me.

'And justice – don't you want to work for justice?' he said.

'Yes, I do,' I said gloomily, 'I want to, but I don't know where it is.'

'And all the blood that has flowed?'

I said nothing, and in the silence Schröter repeated:

'And all the blood that has flowed?'

I looked at the pale, monitory figure in front of me, and at Bruno's battered face, and at the policeman who had come with us and in his good-natured fashion was surprised and puzzled by what was going on.

'There ought to be a country in which one could sleep, do nothing but sleep,' I said.

One afternoon I made my way through Berlin to the station, and at nine o'clock next morning I was on the platform at C., whistling, because I was at home. I had one shabby, sweaty suit, a relatively new overcoat made of grey military material, a pair of stout leather shoes, 500 marks, and the rest of my life in front of me. Suddenly it struck me that I had no idea where to go next. I didn't want to go to the brickworks, and there was nowhere else in the town where they would take me in.

In sheer uncertainty about what to do, I strolled slowly along the embankment next to the railway line, and that is how I made my way through the town. The grey houses, the brick factory buildings

on either side of the track, looked even more
disconsolate than I remembered them. Then I saw
a lean, shrivelled man with bent head and shoulders
walking along. He went into one of the grey houses,
and I stood there staring at the door that shut
behind him.

I don't know how long I stopped there like that.
When I came to myself again I had walked quite a
long way, I had climbed the street up to the
Gablenzer Berg and was standing in front of the
house.

I went in, and bent down and felt for the monogram; the good feeling of being at home again
spread through me from my finger-tips.

In the yard I found a bit of iron. I used it to
remove the cellar door, which I carried on my back
down the street and out into the woods.

Lying on my door, I spent the night in deep,
happy sleep.

OVER THE ROOF-TOPS

THE last place I lived in before I had to leave Leipzig was an attic on the fourth floor of a gloomy letting house in the Sternwartenstrasse. It was not an old house, it cannot have been more than about a hundred years old, but it was completely in the unfriendly style of the neighbourhood, bare and angular, with dark gloomy staircases, the walls of which were covered with dirty patches of fungus from the damp. The yard was three paces wide and six long, the building next door had been burnt out, and the gaping windows and dangling beams emphasised the feeling of inhospitality.

The house had the frailties and anxieties of age without its romance. It was a dark and airless living machine, with a musty cellar smell that went all the way up to the roof, and it had been condemned to death. At the town hall you could inspect the plan that showed in which year it was due for demolition and what the Sternwartenstrasse would look like in the future. But I deplored the prospect of its demolition, because I lived in the attic, from which there was a remarkable view. The houses were closely packed together, a higgledy piggledy herd of dumb animals raising their humps into the sky, and between them the spires pointed upwards just as if they were arms pointing at something.

Life up over the roof-tops was different from life on the floors below. Only on days when it was heavily overcast did the shadowy life of the back-yards and staircases mount up to us, but normally we top-floor tenants were a privileged caste. We had ample air and light. From my dormer window I could reach out into the gutter, in which little islands of earth had gathered and become overgrown with grasses and dandelions. Thus green and yellow patches spread over the roof-tops, as if to establish a garden for the benefit of the sparrows and attic dwellers.

When the sun shone I stretched an ironing board between the table and the window and lay on it, wearing bathing trunks only, and looked out at the gleaming roofs, watched the sparrows, and talked to my landlady's cat, who was the real mistress of the roof-tops and liked coming to see me.

I also had other visitors. At the time of the fair people used to come and see me from distant towns and parts of the country that had grown strange – men whom one had met somewhere or other years ago and perhaps had known for years and women whom once upon a time one had known well. They were always out of breath when they got to the top of the stairs and came in and sat down. So this is where you live, is it? Do you remember the old days? And do you remember so-and-so or when we were at such-and-such? And when they had gone I stood at the dormer window and watched the night creeping up from the earth and down from the sky and laying itself over the roofs. The old days? Oh, yes, the old days. And then the cat came stalking sure-footedly along the gutters. It belonged to my landlady and had no name, it was simply called 'cat.' At first this surprised me, for it is strange to hear a living creature answering to the name of its species.

I confess that after my visitors left I felt almost

a sense of relief. Nothing of the past still existed. I lived in my crow's nest with my view of the roof-tops, with sparrows, the cat and a blind woman for company.

A few days after I moved in my legs began to itch. It must have been in June, when the sun shone and the cat's fleas must have multiplied. It was a long time before I realised what was happening. During the warm weather I wore no socks, and I discovered that the small, dark creatures generally haunted my calves. I examined the cat, and there was no doubt about it, it was full of fleas.

I had no experience with animals. Townsman as I am, this was my first encounter with cat's fleas, and in any case I had never had a cat. It struck me that, as my landlady was blind, she could not see her cat's fleas, and this worried me. In some ways life with the blind is easier than with the sighted, but in others it is tremendously diffi-cult. I broached the subject very cautiously indeed, and when she realised what I was getting at her broad features flushed, and I shamefully dropped my eyes.

She told me that it was very rare indeed for a human being to suffer from animal fleas. It must be because of the unusual composition of my blood, she said; in any case she had never felt anything. The outcome was that some powder was bought and rubbed into the cat, but unfortunately it didn't do any good. The chemist advised me to rub petrol into the floor, and gradually I got rid of the fleas and the cat seemed to feel better, too.

This broke the ice between me and my landlady.

Previously we had exchanged only a few insignificant words, but after our conversation about fleas we got on very well indeed, and a relationship was established to which I owe my freedom.

It began with trifles – writing paper, for instance. How often had I gone from shop to shop and succeeded in getting nothing but the poorest quality, woody paper, but she had no difficulty in getting reams of the best quality. Her wide, empty eye-balls moved even the most boorish shopkeeper to compassion and lured the stuff from under the counter.

As I was writing a great deal at the time, and also wasted sheet after sheet, she soon started calling me paper-eater, which I countered by calling her flea-mother, and on that basis we got on excellently. We lived a life apart from the chaos of those years, in a roof-top paradise high over the streets and acres of rubble; and, as she was born and had spent all her life here in the Seepiepe, she had an endless store of curious tales about the thieves and fences, whores and hussies, rogues and inn-keepers of the neighbourhood, and I could have written a long book about it and its inhabitants.

But what chiefly interested me was the flea-mother herself. She was a sturdy, robust woman nearing her fifties, her voice was harsh and shrill in the upper registers, and her milk-white eye-balls stood out as if in despair at their uselessness, as if to get as close as possible to the things they could not see, to grasp and embrace and discover all about them. I can still visualise her broad and sturdy form

making its way through the narrow alleys of the
Seepiepe in a rather neglected, crumpled dress and
a yellow arm-band secured with two safety pins and
carrying a walking stick with which she investi-
gated the world. She was a blind woman like others
you see every now and then in the street. But was
she really totally blind? There were occasions when
I doubted it, as on the day when the cat fell out of
the window, for instance.

I was sitting at my typewriter when I heard the
loud screech from down in the yard. At first I
thought it was a child. The flea-mother scuttled
out of the kitchen next door and went clattering
down the stairs. What had happened was this. The
cat had jumped on to the kitchen table, attracted
by half a pound of sausage. When the flea-mother
opened the kitchen door it dropped the sausage in
alarm and tried to jump from the table to the
window-ledge, but it misjudged the distance and
went flying out of the window and landed on the
stone paving of the yard four floors below. It got a
bloody nose and limped for a few days, but that
was all. I should not have believed this to be possible, but my landlady's detailed explanation of the
incident surprised me even more. How could a
blind woman have told so exactly what had happened? She could not have seen the cat jumping
from the table and missing the window-ledge.

So I suspected that she was not totally blind.
Once I struck a match right in front of her eyes,
but they remained cold and unresponsive, the
naked eye-balls quivered and strayed inquiringly
this way and that under the lids, but betrayed no

recognition of what was happening. I decided there must be some other explanation. Is it not said of the blind that the loss of their sight reinforces their other senses, refines and over-refines them? Are not deaf or deaf-and-dumb persons, for instance, known to stand with their backs to musical instruments, pianos or harpsichords or cembalos, and sense the musical vibrations?

One evening the flea-mother hesitantly knocked at my door. It was one of those late autumn evenings that fall earlier every day, bringing with them the disillusionments of the ending year.

When I called out, 'Come in,' she put her head round the door and whispered:

'There's a smell of gas.'

I diligently examined all the rooms and the corridor and the stairs outside, but for all my efforts I could not find a trace of gas. To reassure her I suggested that perhaps someone had lit a gas-cooker downstairs; there was often a smell of gas from the Michels on the second floor.

But she obstinately shook her head. Next morning a door in a flat in the house next door was forced open and a man was found with his head in the gas-oven.

You can explain such incidents in any way you like. You can say she had second sight, or you can say that by reason of her exceptionally developed sense of smell she really was able to smell gas through a party wall.

But let me describe how she climbed out on to the roof.

Just above the level of the dormer window there

was a flat area on which one could walk, and it was possible to get access to it by climbing out of the window and up the roof by the side of it. One night the police arrested a whole gang up there without my noticing anything; in fact I slept right through until late next morning. They actually caught six-teen of them, and I was not a little astonished to learn that the gang had been using the roof for months as a secure meeting place, where they planned their coups and divided the spoil. They had used the stairs of our house and the house next door for months without being disturbed, and had duplicate keys for all the doors. The only one to suspect anything had been the blind flea-mother, who got on their trail and spent several nights hidden on the roof listening to them. She later con-fessed to me that she had been very reluctant to call the police, to whom it was not the custom to have recourse in the Seepiepe. In her opinion steal-ing *Schnapps* and cigarettes was better than putting on boots and uniform and going out and killing people, so it was better to let them get on with it. The reason why she ended by calling the police in spite of her principles in the matter was that she discovered that they were graduating to robbery with violence. This, she felt, was going too far.

At first I could not believe this story, and I failed completely to suppress a sceptical grunt, whereupon she put her big hands on my cheeks as if trying to feel my incredulous smile. 'Don't you believe me?' she said. 'Come and see for yourself.'

She went over to the window and climbed out, and I had no choice but to follow her, so we both

climbed up to the roof, and I felt very much
ashamed of myself because I felt giddy while she
went up ahead of me with complete confidence.

When we got there I appreciated properly for the
first time the urban mountain range that the build-
ers had created. It was an undulating labyrinth of
chimneys, bricks and tiles, stucco and ridged roofs,
interlocking buildings that had been demolished,
rebuilt, divided up, or added to. The blind woman
pointed out the gang's meeting-place and showed
me her own place of concealment, but I was still
sceptical and incredulous, and did not suspect how
soon I should need to use it myself. I decided to
write a short story about the Seepiepe and the flea-
mother and this strange world up on the roof-tops.
That was what I decided to do, but what do our
plans and intentions for tomorrow amount to? How
little we know about what is really going to happen
next day. My idyllic life in the attic came ab-
ruptly to an end, perhaps because it is contrary to
justice for a man to live in the roof-tops, almost up
in the sky, without sharing the town's troubles and
the destiny of its inhabitants. Perhaps it is immoral
to write one's private short stories while mankind
is suffering its history. For we were living through
one of those unusually painful periods, a time of
transition between two ages, with great defeats
behind and great errors ahead, an age during which
the powerful of this earth were forging new methods
of violence and destruction.

One evening the flea-mother knocked at my door,
and when I opened it I saw that her face was grey

with fear and her usual cheerful confidence had
vanished. All my questioning failed to elicit what
was on her mind, but she infected me with her
anxiety, and that night I could not sleep, and when
the bell began to ring furiously I fled through the
window to the hiding-place on the roof. From there
I could hear their voices, hoarse, excited male
voices and the loud assurances of the flea-mother. I
stayed quietly in my hide-out all night. At first
light she brought me everything I needed for my
escape. Before I left she pressed my hand. 'Good
luck,' she muttered, and spat three times over her
shoulder. Do you know what gratitude is?

GRATITUDE

HUNGER made my stomach turn and brought tears to my eyes. For two hours I lay watching the silent village. There was no sign of life. I slipped into the first cottage. The windows were smashed and the door open.

I searched three cottages without finding so much as a crust of bread. In the fourth a table was laid, ready for a meal. It was laid very simply. There were no plates and no dishes. There was nothing but an iron pan in the middle, and in it, I could hardly believe my eyes, there was a crisply roasted cold chicken.

I sat down and ate it at one go. When I had finished the door slowly opened and Radionov walked in. He looked at me in amazement, noticed the empty pan, and a wave of anger reddened his good-natured face.

That was how I was taken prisoner.

Radionov, to whom I owe my life, struck me a blow that knocked me off the chair. Then he took me across the yard, where another soldier was passing the time with a woman who was not as young as she had been.

I couldn't understand where all these people had come from so suddenly. The soldier dropped the woman's skirt. I was made to stand against the wall with my hands up.

'What are you doing, *tovarish*?' asked Radionov, to whom I owe my life.

The other soldier raised his pistol. Anger marked his young, round face. He wanted to kill me, kill me out of hand, *prosto*, with no beating about the bush.

Radionov came and stood between us. His face

was pale. 'Just a minute, he's my prisoner,' he said. 'You've been having a good time here with this woman while I've been making war. So this Fritz belongs to me.'

The woman, who had been tensely watching, grabbed the soldier by the sleeve. This made him lose his temper. He shook the woman off and brandished his pistol in Radionov's face.

'What are you going to do with this *nyemets*, then? Are you going to take him away and leave me alone? And what about our orders? I say finish him off, *prosto*.'

Radionov stubbornly shook his head, and his big ears reddened.

'He's my prisoner,' he said, 'and Comrade Stalin's orders are that no more prisoners are to be shot. *Ponimayu*?'

'Comrade Stalin isn't here, is he? Here there's nobody but us.'

'Are you proposing to disobey Stalin's orders? That I can't permit!'

'I don't understand you, Vasily, you didn't behave like this last month, at Shitomir we sent the *nyemtsi* to heaven and you didn't hesitate, Vasily.'

'At that time Comrade Stalin had not yet issued the order,' Radionov said deliberately, with his strong hand killing a fly that landed on his brow.

And Radionov spent a whole day conscientiously escorting me through the sun-baked countryside. When we left the village the other soldier went back to enjoying himself again with the woman. We marched along the road and didn't meet a soul till midday. Then we met three young Poles, and their faces, which were hollowed with hunger and fear, lit up eagerly as they went for me.

I saw that Radionov didn't want to intervene. I defended myself as best I could, but soon I was lying with my face in the dirt. But it soon started getting too lively for Radionov, and he drove the three Poles away. They clenched their fists and swore at him, and he swore back and laughed heartily. My hands and face were bleeding. Radionov gaily fired a shot in the air, and we went on our way, and my gratitude to him passed all bounds.

Gradually the countryside grew less deserted. Soldiers came marching along the road. They marched in disorderly fashion, with bowed heads and dust on their helmets.

One young, fair-haired soldier was singing a song: *Shiroka strana moya rodnaya . . .*

When he caught sight of me his youthful voice stopped short, and an expression of deadly fear flashed across his face. The good-natured Radionov waved to him, and he hesitantly started singing again, and the others joined in, with hollow, muffled voices:

> *Ya drugoi takoi stranui nyesnayu*
> *Gde tak volyen uchen chelovek. . . .*

That was how Radionov marched me along the road, to an accompaniment of swearing and singing. I was struck and kicked, given bread and cigarettes, laughed at and sworn at.

Radionov protected me from maltreatment by

the drivers of some tanks. When the rattling colossi turned up we left the road and cut across the fields.

Then the headquarters building came into sight, and Radionov asked me for my medals. When I put the bits of lead in his hand, he smiled and swore with satisfaction. He could have simply taken them from me, but he was a proud man and asked me for them.

Inside the building I was taken before a group of senior officers. They inquired politely after my health, gave me water to drink, and asked me what I thought of the Soviet Union. I was delighted at being still alive. They clapped me benevolently on the back, and an orderly handed round vodka in the lids of German cooking utensils. They snapped their fingers against their throats, and one of them called out in a harsh Russian accent:

'*A votre santé.*'

And so we drank to German-Soviet friendship. Afterwards two friendly young officers in green caps appeared and took me to a group of trees some distance away. Here I was made to undress, and was dreadfully beaten up.

After that the interrogation began. I thought all the time about Vasily Radionov, who was now on his way back to the front again and could have killed me.

Gratitude caused me scarcely to feel the blows. What are a few blows when your life has been spared? I sang the sad song in praise of their country that Russian soldiers sang on the way to the front:

Ya drugoi takoi stranui nyesnayu
Gde tak volyen uchen chelovek. . . .

I know no other land
Where a man's heart beats so freely. . . .

When it was over a *muzhik* brought me a cooking
utensil full of water. I spat my teeth out on to the
grass, drank the water, looked at the red sky, and
said:

'What luck, I've survived the war.'

MELANCHOLY

IT happened as if it were bound to happen. The reasons may have been metaphysical in nature, but only the grim details could be recorded.

2

Crowded into the yard of an abandoned farm, a party of soldiers were cutting off the heads of a lot of flapping chickens. Near them lay a second lieutenant, his head hidden under his coat and a blanket. His batman crouched over him, trying to wake him up.

Captain Frey, commander of the now barely existent battalion, came stalking across the road. His brown desert breeches billowed over his knees like the sails of a pirate ship; his shoes had been cracked by the stones of the Moncato.

The second lieutenant, torn from his sleep, reeled towards him and reluctantly saluted.

'Take twenty men,' the captain began, and then corrected himself. 'No, we've got to count every single man, take nineteen, that is, twenty including yourself, and make your way to the Moncato and bring down the wounded.'

The second lieutenant, his dream still on his brow, his tired eyes hidden behind his swollen lids, was about to turn away when the captain called him back.

'There's one other thing,' he said. 'The court-martial will sit as soon as things get quiet. You gave the order to retreat and will have to answer for it.

So make good use of tonight, because it may be your last chance, and may make the court more favourably inclined towards you.'

The second lieutenant stood motionless. When he saluted and turned away the red evening sky lay on his shoulders. The decapitated heads of the chickens shrieked in the yard; there was incredible fear in their eyes.

3

The party made off, each man crouching in the purple shadow of the man in front. Over their heads the sky was like a stone as pale as wax. Then the moon mounted over the horizon, climbed steeply over the Cyclopian mountains and cast its lemon light on the summit, from where it fell shriekingly into the ravines. The mountains grew nearer.

The party crept southwards along the infernal valley of the dried up Simeto between Adrano and Paterno.

Three hours passed. In the brushwood on the banks the dead of past battles swung in the night wind. When the men left the stream-bed and began the climb a whisper came from above:

'It's us, don't shoot.'

Second Lieutenant Maraun and his men had reached their destination. In the tracery of the slit trenches their fear mingled with the wounded men's hope.

There was a smell of orange blossom.

The moon was tangibly close, a cold shining
wheel, looking as if you could turn it if you dared.
Because of its pitilessness they puffed greedily at
their cigarettes.

4

The dried-up Simeto lay below, white and
stony. In this part of the world the streams dry up
in spring.

The volcano lay on the northern horizon, hurling
its fire into the sky.

'In case we get separated, the objective is Etna.
The new positions are on the southern slope. The
army is withdrawing to the foot of the volcano.
We'll make it by first light.'

The second lieutenant looked at the fiery cone.
A long way away in the sky an aircraft hummed.
The volcano disgorged blood and death into the
yielding expanse of the night. The wounded swore
softly and threw away their cigarettes; men whispered encouragement to each other. There were
two bearers for each wounded man. Some could be
held by their arms and legs, but others could be
carried only on a man's back. While the bearers
with their loads were on the way down in the darkness a sound came from the dead at the former
company headquarters.

A human form, its face blackened with blood,
moved, and a groan liberated it from the glassy
stare of the others.

This brought the number of wounded to eleven,
and the second lieutenant took charge of him. The

man had been struck in the leg by a shell splinter, and had been lying among the dead as if dead himself.

'Off we go.'

The two were the last living men on the Moncato, on which the moonlight played as if it took pleasure in the stiffened corpses.

5

Second Lieutenant Maraun carried the wounded man on his back. The first stretch downhill was the worst; the grey rock was treacherous in the dark. Each time he stumbled, the man dug his clammy fingers into his neck.

'Steady, steady.'

They fell. The man's weight pressed his face into the earth. He spat out blades of grass and sand, and his saliva and breath were spiced with the taste of blood.

'We'll manage it,' the second lieutenant assured himself and the wounded man.

'Are you going to take me home, sir?' the man said.

'Home? That's a long way away.'

With the stiff burden on his back he clambered downwards, clutching in one hand a leg slippery with blood. When he got half way to the bottom flaming Etna disappeared and the mountains opposite came into view. In the valley of the Simeto the others were waiting for them behind the glimmer of their cigarettes.

6

The fortune of war is capricious and incalculable. The god of war is an arrogant god and distributes luck and ill luck as he thinks fit.

The Moncato had been held and then lost and then retaken.

Then two men had arrived with the news that, with the exception of a handful of wounded left on the mountain with no one to bring them down, No. 3 Company had been wiped out. The battalion commander heard the news like a judgement of fate. Tiredness exploded in his brain. The rocky Moncato hurt his eyes; the vision would haunt him for the rest of his days. There are visions like this which are passed on to the next generation and appear in their dreams. Their father's death scenes.

The battalion commander linked the fate of the wounded with that of Second Lieutenant Maraun. His life was imperilled like theirs; he could save them or perish with them. Only the lucky survive lost battles.

Second Lieutenant Maraun consulted his map in the muffled light of his torch. Wavy lines indicated his chances of successfully extricating himself. The enemy had cleverly and contemptuously ceased to bother about the mountain, and were now advancing north on Etna in a pincer movement right and left.

With his eyes on the flaming mountain, Second Lieutenant Maraun signalled to his men to carry on.

7

A bare hour later their load was lightened by one man. His listless eyes sank deeper and deeper as the life ebbed out of them, and he bled peacefully to death in their hands. The two who had been carrying him laid him on a flat rock and looked at him in perplexity.

Then they went and helped the others. At this point the stream-bed fell away in a series of steep drops. When the rains came there were waterfalls here more than six feet high.

It was here that the fateful conversation took place between Second Lieutenant Maraun and the soft-voiced n.c.o.

8

The stony wilderness was deadly cold. The carriers were engaged in an unequal struggle and were staggering with exhaustion. The wounded cursed their weight, the night, the stream-bed and the war. When the first of them started sobbing aloud the officer with his load on his back struggled over to them, panting, and struck them.

The n.c.o.'s soft voice protested against such pitilessness.

'Half an hour's rest, sir, please.'

The n.c.o. was close in the officer's shadow. His soft-voiced murmur was taken up from man to man. They raised their heads.

'Half an hour, sir, please, just half an hour.'

The officer stopped and listened. Only a few days earlier he had led the company in a senseless assault on a small wood held by tanks, it had been shot to pieces, and he had given the order to withdraw. He had dashed hither and thither among the streams of bullets and ordered the survivors back. It had been the only reasonable course, but now he was going to pay for it by being court-martialled.

He knew what half an hour's rest would mean. It was impossible, there was not even a minute to lose. He went up close to the n.c.o. Their voices dropped to a whisper, and none of the men could hear what they said.

'I'm in command here.'

'The men can't carry on, the wounded are dying on their hands.'

'If we're not behind the lines by first light, we're done for.'

'If we don't have a rest, we're done for in any case.'

'I'm in command here.'

The men flung themselves down on the stones. Why hadn't he been killed in the assault on the wood? 'One doesn't strike a wounded man, sir.' The soft-voiced n.c.o. won. But he hadn't struck the wounded, he had struck the grumbling carriers. He would have to answer for it. But he would have to answer in any case. How could he drive these exhausted men on? They were squatting or lying on the stones, and in the dark you could hardly make them out. 'We're carrying on,' he heard himself say. 'We're carrying on,' he heard himself repeating. No one moved and everything remained

still, so he looked for the n.c.o. 'We're going on,'
he said, pressing the muzzle of his pistol into the
n.c.o.'s flesh.

The n.c.o. sat up.

'So we're going on,' he mumbled.

'No,' said the officer.

'We're not going on?'

'Stay where you are and rest.'

He moved aside. He noted with surprise a numb-
ness coming over him, a dark, irresistible, warming
feeling of ceasing to care, and it was almost with
satisfaction that he felt the time passing. He felt a
sweet kind of painfulness, as if his blood were ebbing away. He raised his eyes and gazed at the starry
sky. Suddenly everything seemed to him to be
different, and a great deal of time was wasted in
this way.

Then a murmur arose, and the men started
moving off. They left two dead bodies behind. The
officer took no notice of them, but the n.c.o. flashed
his dimmed torch in their eyes and, as they were
beyond aid, the men who had been carrying them
were free to take turns with the others.

After this they made better progress. But they
were still only half way when dawn came treacher-
ously over the hills and the war started up again.

9

They should have passed the railway bridge
under cover of darkness, and when they tried to
find a way round it they were machine-gunned by
some grinning New Zealanders. The carriers put

down the wounded and sprang aside. The officer
idiotically put his hand to his cap and began running through the olive groves and vineyards with
his load on his back. Just before a walled-in water-
course he collapsed. The two men lay and put
their hands and faces into the meagre flow that was
used to irrigate the vineyard.

They lapped up the water and moaned happily.

10

Broad daylight came and the sun prepared for its
pitiless course. To the north was Etna, its lightly
ringed smoke signal rising straight into the sky like
a candle. Maraun looked at it, and then at his
compass.

'What's your name?' he asked his companion.

'Walter Bölisch.'

'Where do you come from?'

'Bamberg.'

He examined the man's wounded leg, adjusted
the bloodstained bandage, and pulled off his shirt
and wrapped it round it.

Inside him there was a murderous mixture of
contempt and determination. He picked the man
up again and set his face to Etna as if he were
greeting it and its smoke signal. I'm coming, he
seemed to say.

11

As he panted up the hill he began talking to his
companion.

'We'll get through, don't you worry,' he said. 'Is your Bamberg a beautiful town? Grit your teeth.'

The man tried to make things as easy as possible for him.

'Yes, it is a beautiful town, you must come and see me there some time. The war's over for me. I am gritting my teeth.'

'We must take care not to fall into a trap.'

'I'm keeping my eyes open.'

'Are you married?'

'Yes. Two children, a boy and a girl.'

'If they spot us, you mustn't hold on whatever you do. I'll simply let you slip to the ground so that I can shoot. Do you understand? Whatever happens I shan't leave you in the lurch. I'm not a man for jokes of that kind.'

'No, you're not.'

Anxiously the man tried to make himself as light as possible on Maraun's back.

12

In the thick brushwood half way up a hill they came to a narrow path. Maraun let the man down and sat beside him. They looked uncertainly at the way ahead, and when they heard somebody coming they lay flat on the ground.

An aged Sicilian passed by, in black ragged trousers and torn shirt. He had a grey, tangled beard and tired eyes.

He walked unhurriedly, carrying a jug in his hand. When he had gone Maraun stood up.

'Stay here,' he said, 'I'll be coming back.'

He wanted to follow the old man, but Bölisch started whimpering.

'You're going to leave me.'

'I'm not going to leave you.'

'Then give me your sub-machine gun.'

Maraun crept back into the undergrowth and laid the weapon at the man's side.

'I'm not up to any monkey business.'

He took his pistol from his belt and released the safety catch.

'If you are, I'll kill you,' said the wounded man.

Maraun failed to catch up with the old Sicilian. He walked along the path with imprudent speed, but the man had vanished. He walked back a little way, and thought he heard the sound of breathing.

Not twenty paces off the path he came upon a primitive dwelling. The Sicilian was sitting on a stone in front of it, holding the jug to his lips.

Maraun emerged from the bushes. The old man went on drinking thoughtfully and with a trace of greed on his features, but his tired eyes watched the foreign soldier with no sign of fear or surprise. Maraun walked past him into the hut. In the semi-darkness he made out a table, a chair and a bed, on which a girl was lying huddled in a coat or blanket. She had muscular legs and black hair.

'*Buon giorno,*' Maraun muttered, retreating into the open air. The old man had put down the jug and was waiting. Something moved on the other side of the hut. Maraun raised his pistol and cautiously looked over the wall, where a kind of stall had been rigged up. He saw the motionless head of a donkey. His first thought was that it was dead, but then it moved, and once more he heard the sound of breathing.

Cautiously he climbed over the rubbish with which the ground was cluttered and took the donkey by the neck. It followed him obediently.

'I'm taking it, I need it for a wounded comrade,' he said. The old man promptly turned into a flapping bundle of hands, he knelt among the stones and thorns, and his limbs quivered as if he had convulsions.

'*Madonna mia, madonna mia,*' he said.

'I can't leave my comrade in the lurch.'

'*Camerata, camerata . . . . .*'

Equally suddenly he changed back again. A tired old man got up from the ground and disappeared into the hut.

'*Avanti, avanti.*'

The donkey took one step, and stopped. Then it took two steps and stopped again. Maraun stuck his pistol into his belly. The donkey stood there as if it were considering the situation, but did not move.

13

Maraun grabbed its head.

Suddenly it started moving. Maraun sighed with relief, but then swung round with his pistol ready to fire. The girl from inside the hut was walking behind them. The face under her shock of black hair was dirty, her features were pinched, her dress stained with earth and vegetation. She tugged at the donkey's tail, and it quickened its pace.

14

The girl helped vigorously to put the wounded man on the donkey, and he groaned with pain. 'Steady, keep a grip on yourself,' said the officer. 'What has got to be done has got to be done.'

The wounded man went on groaning, and Maraun got angry with him, and so he remained until the groans subsided to a whimper. Then he hung the sub-machine gun over the man's chest and told him to keep a good look-out and, if he saw anybody coming, to be sure to fire first.

The wounded man gazed ahead with reddened, feverish eyes. Maraun brought up the rear with his pistol at the ready.

The girl had got herself a stick and kept the donkey going without any trouble. When they stopped for a breather she patted the creature's neck, but her features remained hard.

The little group was surrounded by repulsive flies and the smell of sweat.

15

The sky formed a red vault over the mountains. The vineyards breathed abandonment, and then night descended from the heights and the black flag over Etna grew bright, like a sign-post showing the way to Sicilians and foreign soldiers.

When they passed through brushwood as tall as a man the wounded man cried out with pain, for the vegetation tore at his wounded leg. From time to time a long-drawn '*Via*' came from the girl's lips as she called the donkey to quicken its pace. For a few moments it did so, only to relapse again into its usual sleepy stride.

'You'll live to curse your Bamberg again,' the officer said with a deprecatory gesture. 'Always stuck in the same old dreary place. You'll look back longingly to the romantic mountains of Sicily.'

He ordered a halt. The girl and the donkey stood still. Cautiously he lifted the wounded man down to the ground. He opened his water bottle and went off to look for water.

'My God, she's running away,' the wounded man cried out.

The officer hurried back. The crackling on the undergrowth betrayed her. He struck her at the back of the neck and listened in the silence. He raised his head and sniffed. All remained quiet. The donkey stood motionless, its ears drooping sadly.

'I'll shoot her down,' the wounded man said.

Maraun put him on the animal's back.

16

During the second night the wounded man's head fell forward sleepily, his back bent, and his arms fell round the donkey's neck.

The ghostly pillar of fire grew nearer, and the acrid smell of the volcano filled the landscape. Maraun said to the girl: 'For you the war will soon be over. My comrade will go to hospital, and you'll

get on your donkey and ride home to papa. That's
why the old gentleman sent you with us.'

She took his hand and laid it on the wounded
man's brow. It had been all for nothing. The man
from Bamberg had set out on a route on which
there were no more hospitals.

For the first time the second lieutenant strangled
something like a sob. Later he removed the strap
from the sub-machine gun and used it to strap the
dying man securely to the donkey's back. The girl
watched attentively. Then she picked some grasses,
plaited them together, and tied the man's legs with
them, caressing the donkey's belly with her cheeks
as she did so.

Then, their package tied up like this, they went
on their way. The girl led the donkey, and the man
died quietly on it. Behind them plodded a brood-
ing second lieutenant, the life gradually departing
from him.

The first thing to leave him was his fear, fear of
the court-martial, military regulations, and death.

After all trace of it had gone, prudence began
leaving him, too, and his features, distorted by
night and depression, grew friendly.

He did not know how long they went on like this,
but suddenly he woke up again, and looked at
the dead man in astonishment.

'Take the donkey and turn round and go home,'
he said.

The girl looked at him.

He pointed southwards.

She turned the donkey round and then stopped.
The officer nodded encouragingly. She walked up

to him. 'Come too,' she said, grabbing his arm. 'Come too, soldier, that way there's peace. Come too.'

Her efforts were in vain.

Absent-mindedly he sought for Italian words, but could not find them, so gave it up and plodded off northwards, in the direction of Etna, relapsing again into his hopeless dream. The dead man swayed about on the donkey's back as the girl made it hurry to catch up with him.

17

Walking as in a dream, they failed to reply to the challenge from the first German post, and the girl, riddled by a burst, collapsed next to the donkey, which halted indifferently. The second lieutenant, with a vague, crazed smile on his face, picked her up and sat her behind the dead man.

The strange procession then continued its way past the astonished steel-helmeted soldiers towards the pillar of fire of Etna.

In the silence that followed the fatal burst the girl's bloodstained body swayed and fell in the road with a thud, and the second lieutenant with his hand in the donkey's meagre mane plodded on without turning his head.

18

Two months later he was shot before daybreak in front of the stone wall of the military prison at Verona. According to the indictment at his court-martial, he had twice been guilty of cowardice in the face of the enemy. The decisive evidence against him was that of an n.c.o., who said in a soft voice that instead of standing his ground he had run away and let his men be shot up.

The n.c.o., who had three bullets in his body and had managed to escape the holocaust in his own way, was the only one ultimately to survive. He gave his evidence at the court-martial held together by triumphant white bandages.

When the second lieutenant was fetched from his cell for his last walk we hammered on the door with our fists.

CAPTAIN ROSTOV

My memory lies in wait for me, crouching like an enemy ready to pounce. A particular shade of light or sound or a smell is sufficient to set it off. It is a fearful weapon, like a dagger poised to strike, or the insidious hand that aims it or casually drops poison into the cup, a small dose only, just a little every day, causing you gradually to waste away, so that each day you are just a little less alive. Memories can kill. I know men who flee from them as from a murderer.

There are various ways of dying of one's memory. Some remember only in sleep. 'I slept badly,' they say when they wake up in the morning, and their faces are as pale as the figures in dreams.

Those are the people whom memory assaults only in bed. As soon as they have got up and returned to the perpendicular it slips away from them; they wash away their dreams, to them it is a mere question of washing and dressing. I admire those people. They open their eyes, and time is subject to them. How lucky they are, how simple everything is to them, as long as they are awake.

But I am a victim of my memories. For five years now I have bolted and barred my bedroom door and ensconsed myself within, permitting no one, not even my wife and children, to come and wake me in the morning. For, if there is anyone bending over me when I awake, it is not my wife's familiar face that I see or the timid voices of my children that I hear, but the crude oaths and irascible features of the person who woke me early one morning, no, it was not early morning, it was still night.

The room I slept in at the time – it was soon

after the end of the war – was feebly lit by an electric light bulb obscured by fly droppings, and the person who woke me was Captain Rostov, of the glorious Red Army, a wild and forceful man with gestures so emphatic that one could draw them. He brought me back to reality in the most brutal fashion. 'At this time of night?' I muttered, and fear filled my mouth like ice-cold water and flowed down into my chest and belly, making me speechless and awake.

The jeep was waiting outside. He switched on the head lights, did something to the engine, and then stepped back. The sulphurous light flooded his crude features and gave them a spectral beauty. My heart thumped all the way up into my throat. I took my place in the jeep beside him, and we drove with howling engine through the dead town and out into the Harth woods, which in the day-time formed a dark patch on the horizon.

The summer night was cold, and I turned up my coat collar. The factory chimneys flared behind us and the clashing of trucks being shunted came from the railway line. The yellow fingers of the searchlights played over the airfield to the south. It was a night devoid of human beings but full of the signs of them, and Captain Rostov in his olive-green Red Army jeep took me to the place of execution, a sandy, circular expanse where Horch, Audi and DKW test drivers had used to try out their latest models.

Captain Rostov got out, squatted on the damp ground, took two bottles of vodka from his *litevka*, and roughly gave me an order.

'Talk about Gitler,' he said.

I looked down at him as he sat there on the ground, for now I towered over him and was looking down on his big bald patch – I could have picked up a stone and smashed in his skull.

He repeated his order.

'Come on, talk about Gitler.'

The sky overhead was gradually assuming its ashen morning face, and under it the town lay like a dark wrinkle in the distant south-east. I looked at it longingly. Smoke rose and encompassed the houses. Near us it grew light, and the outline of the fir-trees emerged cautiously from the dark.

Rostov had once been aide-de-camp to the Soviet Marshal Blucher. When Blucher was shot Colonel Rostov was deprived of his rank and vanished to a camp in Siberia. In the Second World War he served in the ranks and worked his way up to captain again.

It was in this capacity that he escorted those condemned to death to the place of execution in the sandpits of the Harth, and it was at this spot where we were now sitting that they put a *makhorka* cigarette between their lips in the grey light of morning, tied a dirty bandage over their eyes, and fired a volley into their hearts.

Captain Rostov, a bow-legged Cossack who had met Lenin, could talk about the chaos of the Russian civil war as if it were yesterday, and drank vodka like water. He and his horrid friendship filled me with wonder and repulsion.

'Come on, talk about Gitler.'

He sat facing me in the early morning light, with the first glow of sunlight on his face.

'Talk about Gitler, come on.'

I was plunged in mist. I remembered ancient legends. I could see Rostov on the back of a galloping horse, a glittering sabre in his strong, leathery hands.

I began telling him about Gitler.

I had seen him twice. The first time I was still a schoolboy, and he came to Meerane and Glauchau for the opening of the *Autobahn*. The second time I saw him I was a soldier, we presented arms, and he crept past with bent shoulders, a vile, nervous man, with envy, hate and doom in his eyes. I often wonder why no one shot him down. No one dared. Also, perhaps, no one thought of it. Even the bravest did not dare. The man who laid his brief-case with a bomb inside it at his feet hurried quickly away. There are faces so horrible that they are not to be borne. Why did no one draw a pistol and shoot him in the brow? He was surrounded by marshals, generals and orderlies. A century before simple soldiers had sacrificed themselves. The private soldier Klinke blew himself up with the Düppel entrenchments, and assured the Prussian victory. Why were there no Germans who sacrificed themselves for millions of their fellow-countrymen? Was it cowardice? Is it cowardice if men allow themselves to be killed instead of killing the man who orders them to kill? No, Captain Rostov, it is not cowardice, and Count Stauffenberg, who placed the bomb, had ten years before been an enthusiastic follower of Hitler's, and he had let himself be shot and crippled for his sake. An officer with a golden wound stripe, a mutilated cripple, a lonely hero, finally dared, and failed. I fell silent. In Rostov's oblique eyes, through which one could see into his wounded Cossack soul, there was the drunken sobriety of the great drinker.

We drank ourselves into a stupor. Through clouds of mist I watched Rostov get up and shake the splintered, bloodstained stake against which those sentenced to death ended their lives.

Rostov stood there, swearing and shouting the name up into the lofty, dancing sky. I emptied the dregs from the bottle on to the earth, which accepted them passively. I began feeling sick and gasping for air. We went over to the brook, looked at it blearily, and lay down in it. The water was ice-cold, but I was trembling with heat. Never had I seen so plainly how evil life was. Never had I seen so plainly how precious it was.

By now it was broad daylight. The woods were steaming. We shook ourselves. A rusty red sun climbed into the sky. To the south-east the mines spewed up dirty clouds over Zwickau. I wanted to tell Rostov that Germans and Russians were brothers, but didn't. I just stared tongue-tied at the stake stuck like a blackened finger into the earth.

Then I vomited.

I was not the only one whom Rostov fetched at night and took to the place of execution and questioned about Hitler; he took plenty of others there too.

That summer I did not see him again, but I met

him at the Robert Schumann House in the autumn. He was busily and gloomily taking photographs. We had some drinks, of course, and he ended by telling me why he took so much interest in Hitler. It was because the condemned men, facing the firing squad at the last moment, nearly always summoned up their strength and defiantly shouted *Heil Hitler*.

Rostov was very pale when he told me this, and he looked at me with an expression of suspicion and disgust.

'My people are not evil,' I said, 'at any rate, they are not more evil than yours, and I hope you realise how much desperation there must be behind a man's calling out *Heil Hitler* two years after the end of the war.'

Rostov would not accept this. He said they were Fascists, wild, stupid and incorrigible Fascists. Why couldn't they say goodbye to the world decently, with a goodbye of a good-night or an oath, if you like, or a word of farewell to their family, or even with *Deutschland über Alles*, so far as he was concerned? But no, they shouted *Heil Hitler*, *Heil Hitler*.

He staggered to his feet, stuck out his arm, and went on shouting *Heil Gitler*, *Heil Gitler*. Then he fell back, exhausted.

I replied that it was all that was left to them, for everything else had been taken away; prison and death sentence had expunged all their disillusion and remorse. When they were taken out into the woods and bound to the stake, they were utterly alone and abandoned by all the gods, and the only thing left to them was that cry of doom. So complete has been your victory, I said to Captain Rostov, that if your enemies are not to die dishonourably they are bound to name that name . . .

I do not know if he understood all that I said, but he threatened me, first with his fist, and then with his pistol, and then he went for the others who gathered round us.

I jumped through the window and out into the street, and walked away feeling guilty and not at all pleased with myself.

Next day I was told that he had been overpowered, beaten up, and dumped in a pit. His pistol found its way by some secret route to the police, who handed it over to the Russian military authorities. Perhaps it was this incident that led to his arrest, and I hope to no more serious consequences. This Old Bolshevik and civil war veteran was, I think, a sensitive human being at heart, and his continuous excesses were his way of reacting to the killing that our two countries demanded of us.

I never saw him again.

Schikora, who worked at the main station, telephoned early one morning and told me that he had just been brought there by a heavily armed Russian escort. I hurried there, but the platform where prisoners were entrained was empty.

'The train has just gone,' the man with the red cap told me, standing with his flag under his arm on the desolate platform, pulling contentedly at his glimmering *makhorka* cigarette.

Seeing my eyes on it, he said: 'A Russian officer

gave it to me. They were taking him away. These are hard times, aren't they?'

I thought about Rostov. The wind was blowing up from Bohemia, leaping high into the sky over the Erzgebirge and clearing away the clouds. The glittering sun, the extinguished eye of God, rolled noisily overhead. I suddenly felt that I had been standing on the platform for years.

I looked round, but there was no one in sight except the railwayman in front of me. With an embarrassed smile on his face he was cramming the cigarette I had wanted to ask him for into his pipe. Suddenly he looked up at me in surprise.

'He was a friend of yours, wasn't he?'

'He was present when they shot my father.'

'Oh,' the man said casually, 'and why did they shoot your father?'

'Because my father shot Russian fathers during the war.'

THE UNSAID PRAYER

LYING under the pine-tree, I looked up at the alien sky. The tree was huge and ancient; its tough, twisted branches monstrously embraced the pale blue vault of heaven, stabbed its tender flesh with its prickly arms, wounded the white, young clouds, sucked blood out of the silence.

At noon the tree conceded defeat. Wind came whistling over the plain. The beech-trees by the river defended themselves reluctantly, their leaves glistening. The gale drove bright light ahead of it; the light leapt down into the leaves of the branches and back again into the first clusters of cloud. For a moment it seemed as if the world had been set alight. The bright light was painful, and I left my pine-tree and sheltered from the brightness in the brushwood on the river bank. I lay in the darkness of the bushes until the world outside had changed. The storm led without transition to night. The darkness was brutal. I lay on my back face upwards and let the rain drip into my open mouth.

The weather had been hot, and I was thirsty. I swam the river, trying to catch fish with my bare hands.

A last flash of lightning lit up the night, harshly illuminating the opposite bank; and white human faces looked aslant at me. Shots rang out in the dark. I was still thirsty, and I plunged in and drank, feeling grateful to the river for enabling me to carry on. I was working my way back to the front. I had been cut off from my unit and overrun by the advancing Russians. At night I walked westward. I knew that the German armies had been beaten, just as I knew that I should never let myself be taken prisoner. During the day I crept into the woods, and walked only at night. I kept myself going on potatoes and turnips from the fields. At the edge of a field I found a rifle, with bayonet fixed. So, I made my way westward, with bayonet fixed, in the direction of the retreating front and, crazed with hunger, I entered a village.

'Bread,' I said, holding the bayonet to the old man's belly. He gave me some bread, and I chewed it greedily as I hurried off towards the wood, brandishing my rifle. The closer I got to the front, the more animated the countryside became. Russian and Polish troops were swarming everywhere, and my uniform grew more and more dangerous to me. I spent two days by the side of a lake, but could not manage to steal one of the bathing soldiers' uniforms.

While I was hunting for berries in the undergrowth I heard footsteps approaching. They were those of a Russian soldier. Perhaps he had seen me and was looking for me.

Less than ten paces away from me, under a spreading oak tree, he took off his *litevka*, carefully spread it on the ground, and quietly sat down with his back to me.

I could see the muscles playing at the back of his neck. The man was eating. Something inside made me feel I ought to give him a chance, but if I called out to him he would turn and I should have to shoot. He might shriek. It would have to be done quietly. But he did hear something, he raised his shoulders and was about to turn, and I stumbled at the last moment and ran the bayonet into his

R.D.—7

back as I fell. The bayonet went in on the left with a grating sound and penetrated heart and ribs.

You would never believe how quietly men can kill. All he let out was an astonished 'Why?' In his *litevka* I found a German pay-book and a wallet with some photographs. I recognised him in some of them. In one of them he was standing with his wife and two daughters in front of a portico, waving his hat, and in another he was sitting at the wheel of a DKW, smiling and showing his teeth.

I pulled off his boots and trousers and washed his bloodstained shirt in the lake.

Afterwards, disguised as a Russian, I could afford to show myself more openly.

All the same, it was unpleasant to have killed a German. But he was in Russian uniform, and how was I to know he was a German? Now I looked like a Russian myself.

The whole thing was an accident. In ordinary times you can spend a long time philosophising about that sort of thing, but when it's a matter of life or death you look after your own skin, and questions of right or wrong or guilt and innocence only make you unable to defend yourself. The only question is whether I shall report the incident when I get back to the German lines. But it doesn't do a dead man's next of kin any good to be told he was killed by his own side. No, I'll say nothing whatever about it, or I'll just report that I came across his dead body. When the war's over they'll put his name on the local war memorial and every year on remembrance day his next of kin will come and lay wreaths and flowers at its foot. I shall tell no one how he died.

I put my own clothes on him and dug him a meagre hole in the undergrowth, so that at least the rats should not get at him. Also I wanted to say a prayer, but couldn't think of one.

ANNA OF BOHEMIA

HER father was a small cottager, neither richer nor poorer than the others; in other words, he was poor. But he was an honest man, and whenever there was a building to be put up he took his axe and saw and made the roof timbers. Every cottager had his trade, but it did not bring in very much, because this was the Bohemian Forest, where life was hard.

Everything that happened flowed naturally from what preceded. In the evening she went to fetch the two goats from the field. She tripped lightly through the undergrowth, as if driven by the wind; the cottage stood apart from the village, and wood and copses lay in between, but she was not afraid. Later, when she had almost forgotten her name and was known to everyone as Anna, she often used to lie awake at night and hear the forest about her, and the owl proclaiming its discontents. Her early memories remained with her, her father telling her she must do what she was told without answering back and thrashing her when she didn't get a good enough price for the milk. 'Drink it yourself,' he used to tell her angrily, and that indeed is what she did, because she liked milk, and went on liking it for the rest of her life. In fact she drank milk as other women drink coffee or men drink beer or *Schnapps*.

One morning she climbed out through the window and started walking north, and kept on walking for many days. At night she took shelter in the woods, and she came upon ravines and juniper trees and mountain ash and great woods of fir and pine, and all these familiar things accom-

panied her on her way. She spent one night by the
smooth trunk of a copper-beech and the next in
the shelter of a wall, and in the morning she saw
the churchyard behind it. When she had finished
the steep climb up from Bohemia and reached the
crest of the Erzgebirge, she came upon an innkeeper standing at the door of his inn. He stood
there quite still, looked up into the grey sky, and
ended by saying:

'And where are you going?'

She stopped and thought, and realised properly
for the first time that she had run away from home.
What was she to say? That she was hungry and
thirsty? That she wasn't tired, because she slept
in the woods, and wanted to continue her way over
the mountains, like hundreds of thousands of
migrants to Saxony who had preceded and would
follow her? That she came from a poor country
and wanted to go to a rich one?

She said nothing, because she didn't know what
to say, so she stayed there for three days, until the
innkeeper threw her out. She worked for him
without asking for pay, but he wanted to take her
into his bed. Before she left she went round to the
back of the inn, climbed into the storeroom, and
drank the cream. The poor and children are
innocent, her father had often said. She wandered
through Saxony. The woods retreated. Poles and
Bohemians worked in the fields under the super-
vision of pale-faced bailiffs riding bad-tempered
horses. Here the air smelled differently, and in the
morning when she went to the factory the sky was
grey, and in the evening when she left it was

invisible. After three years she still felt the paternal
thrashings when she drank milk, and she drank
half a litre daily. She never wrote home. Once,
after she had gone into the milk business, she
scribbled a few lines on a sheet of paper, but she
never posted it.

She collected milk from the villagers and took
it to the town, using a small cart drawn by dogs;
she was the first woman milkman in our neighbourhood. On her rounds she sang songs that nobody
understood, Bohemian songs about forest trees
that climbed up to heaven, and about the two
dwarfs, and about night-flying owls.

Anna, as she was now called by everybody, was a
tough girl. Strong winds blow down from the
mountains in these parts, and the winters are cold,
and there were times when the milk froze in the
cans, but the frost and the long spring rains did not
worry her. She fetched the milk and sang, and she
got married and had three children. Her husband
came from Bohemia, too, and his name was
Thaddeus, but she rechristened him Ernst. He had
never spent more than four weeks under the same
roof, but Anna tamed him. She had saved some
money, and they rented a small brickworks,
because Ernst was a brick-maker by trade.

As wife and mother she spared neither herself
nor others. She cut up the clay, put it in the forms,
and loaded the hard-baked bricks into the lorries.
She sang only rarely now, and in her hard, faulty
German kept the children in order, told them to
do what they were told without answering back,
and imparted to them the ancient wisdom of her

Bohemian father, namely, that no debt should ever be left unpaid, whether for good or evil.

Sometimes in the brief, niggardly evening she talked about the big forest that surrounded her house at home and climbed up to the sky. There was not much sky there, but it shone brightly.

In many ways she was still a little girl. She drank milk every day sitting with the muscular, sunburnt, beer-drinking brickmakers, whom she watched suspiciously and sent back to work punctually at the precise minute.

On February 3, 1933, two policemen appeared whose faces she never forgot. She never forgot how Ernst turned and waved to her at the bottom of the path just by the barn. That was the last time she saw him, and afterwards she walked down the path to the barn every day and saw her husband being taken away by two uniformed men, limping slightly, almost imperceptibly, because he had been shot in the leg on the Isonzo in the First World War.

In those years her Bohemian childhood must have revived in her. Grief is a shadow that sinks into the heart.

Her business flourished, and the brickworks grew. There was a big demand for bricks, but sometimes she sent the workers home. The mechanical press stood still, and no sound came from the lime-pit. But no letter went to Bohemia even now.

Then there were no more brick-makers, no more men who stood in front of the furnace with bare chests and leather on their hands to protect them from the sizzling heat, no more men who could drink fantastic quantities of beer and yet remain sober. All of them marched off enthusiastically to other countries, and went to their death bursting with health and bulging with muscles, and her sons went with them. Only Anna was left, standing alone in the cold dark passages in front of the shelves on which there were no more bricks.

A fortnight before the end of war the place was broken into, and next morning the door of the shed hung askew on its hinges and the goats had gone. After this Anna had to walk to the village two and a half miles away to fetch her milk every morning. She had drunk milk as long as she could remember. The Americans arrived, Negro troops dashed up and down the road in dusty jeeps, and Anna had to walk in the gutter, two and a half miles there and two and a half miles back. It was flat country, and no trees grew here, but sometimes she felt she was walking through the Bohemian Forest.

Then the Negroes drove off to the west and troops from the east moved in, a unit from the Caucasus. They were dirty and unkempt, and came with creaking carts. Anna was on her way back from the village, with the milk splashing about in her milk can, and she realised what they wanted only when she was on her back. She concentrated on one thing; her right hand clung protectively to her milk can, which she held far enough away to prevent it from being upset and near enough to be able to hold it firmly.

Later, alone in the brickworks, she sat on the

green wooden bench in front of the furnace, a lonely old woman who drank milk, and the town was filled with the short, hoarse cries of the men from the Caucasus.

The town commandant was named Kolya. He had a saucy black moustache and his movements were quick and uncontrolled. He wore his black and red Cossack cap with a cross on it askew on his clean-shaven head, on which it sat both firmly and loosely, just like the pistol in his hands. He sang and drank and shot, and swore as only Cossacks swear.

To the town he was both god and devil; he punished and pardoned, let live and die, distributed property and money and clothes, and dashed through the narrow streets in his death-dealing jeep.

On an evening in July she came to Kolya and said to him: Here you are, you Russians, who have come from the ends of the earth with creaking carts drawn by small, dwarf horses. Here you are, you Russians, and the road was full of you and now the streets of the town are full of you, and you, Cossack commandant, are the commander of troops who rape old women. You come from the Caucasus and you, commandant, come from a steppe that to us is nameless, and what do you bring?

The commandant looked at her thoughtfully, and said: You are no German; and he pushed a bottle towards her. But she said that all her life she had drunk nothing but milk.

Only milk, my son, she said, pure, fresh milk,

and the words made her uselessly young again,
turned her into the girl who had run away from
Bohemia and come to Saxony, and it all flashed
through her mind again. *Mleko*, she said, give me
milk, commandant, and he, like a god to whom
nothing was impossible, caused milk to be brought.
And she said: *Tovarish*, you come from the
steppes, and what do you bring? Listen to the
screams and look at the fiery glow in the sky. And
what is it that you ought to bring? The International, I say. Where is the International, commandant? Under the cap on your bald head,
perhaps? Or have you hidden it under your shirt?
Was it the International that your men showed me
on the road?

And the commandant answered, and said: The
International that I bring you, Hussite woman, is
that of slit bellies and decapitated bodies. You
know it, and your men know it, it was they that
taught us it, and we shall never forget it. They took
it all the way to the steppes and look, my hands are
still red with it.

But he had narrow, white hands, and also he
was unusually well educated, and he said: How is
it that you, Hussite woman, know that that other
International ought to exist?

I know what ought to be, she replied, but I am
not one to leave a debt unpaid.

Next morning the commandant's jeep was
waiting outside the town hall, and two soldiers
arrived with a man in their midst carrying a bundle.
Kolya, the commandant, took the wheel, Anna got
in next to him, and the jeep howled off to the

brickworks outside the town. There they stopped, and the civilian had to undo the bundle and change his clothes.

It's your uniform, they said, it fits you perfectly.

Then the two young Russians took the German police officer in their midst, and his proud face was encrusted with blood and dirt. They walked down the path, and Anna called out: Don't forget, stop at the barn and wave.

He stopped at the barn, and waved goodbye to life.

Kolya, the commandant, with his Cossack cap drawn low over his brow, drew his pistol with a significant gesture.

Woman, this means death, he said. You will not be able to stay in the town, they'll kill you.

She laughed, and then her voice grew soft. Let me tell you a story, commandant, she said, about a man and a woman who had a small, dog-drawn cart. Year after year they used it to fetch milk from the villages to the town, and one morning the woman was left alone. And, as before, she fetched the milk from the villages, and her eyes were blind with grief, and she handed out the milk at 21 pfennigs a litre, which was the price, and the women took the milk in jugs and cans and gave it to their children and their husbands to drink, and the milk was red. The town drank my husband's blood.

The commandant put his pistol back in the holster. He thirsted for justice at that moment.

As long as I live, he muttered, they will get what they gave, and his body hunched as if with cramp as he stood with his back to the east. And he said to himself: The thousand roads that lead from my home to yours are full of the empty boots of the dead, and blood and tears flow into them.

He straightened himself, and flung his Cossack cap into the air. Down by the barn the soldiers pushed the waving man up against the wall and shot him dead.

When his expressionless, murderous face hit the ground the jeep with Kolya at the wheel roared off back to the town.

But Anna walked off towards the south, taking the way by which the Hussites had come, and she took everything back, the forest in which she had spent her childhood, the cemeteries to which she had been indifferent, and her revenge – no debt must ever be left unpaid. She made her way over mountains and between armies deep into Bohemia, where the house was in which they lived. And she remembered them as if time had stopped still and nothing had changed. Would not her barefooted little brothers and sisters who were now included in that great, longed for, International which Ernst had used to talk about come running towards her?

The house was empty, the doors open, the windows smashed, and on the hearth there lay an old man with his skull smashed in and, what with his age and the blood, there was no telling whether she would have been able to recognise him.

SONG FROM HEAVEN
OVER REMAGEN

SOMETIMES I get right outside myself. It's an indescribable process, and it still fills me with amazement and incredulity, but the evening smells of musk, and the red and blue trail of sunset hands over Remagen across the river and cries aloud of transience.

I came here two years ago, a stranger, and stood on the bank of the Rhine and looked across to Remagen, and something turned in my stomach like the barrel of an old hurdy-gurdy, the shafts were pointed and tickled the walls of my stomach. Men are no saints. At all events I want to cry out when it hurts and dance when the world turns. The man who was knocked down a few days ago on the bend near Kropelin was no saint either, and I distinctly felt the barrel turning in my stomach. Later it said in the paper that his name was Heinz Magerle, but by that time he was stiff and cold and no longer lay on the bend near Kropelin, agonisingly clawing at the black skin of the asphalt.

Drive a ten-inch nail into your skull and hang your hat on it was what Uncle Brock always used to say, but for the past two years he has been rotting in the prison cemetery at Canndorf and his flesh has been rising as sap in the stunted alders, and the barrel organ has been turning in my stomach, going ding-dong, ding-dong. The axis of the world passes through everyone's body, and in some you can detect it from the way their eyes twitch.

Gargantua crept out of his mother's ear, because she had eaten too much tripe. *Ave virgo, mater Christi, quae per aurem concepisti.* But Uncle Brock used to say that we all emerged from Germania's backside, so were no better than dung.

Gaudeamus igitur. Let us sing our imprecations.

Generations sank blaspheming into the grave, and the coffin-makers have nimble fingers. Down with death. Death is a myth, a dream, a pretence, a magician's wand, an eye knocked out of its socket, a stupid thing that everyone talks of and nobody knows anything about. Death is a middle-rank official in a senior position subject to dismissal at a month's notice, and should be allowed no more scope. Let us give him notice and get rid of him, he has no trade union card, he's absurd and stupid, old-fashioned and voracious, so let's kill him, because he killed my Uncle Brock, the last man who had earth in his blood and a voice like a September fog and a thirst like the sea that drinks up all the rivers.

He had his own peculiar views about life, and death, and hell, which everyone knows, and heaven, which nobody knows, and the earth, which we all pollute. When he had been drinking he started talking. A lot of people say he was crazy, and he may have been, but what of it?

There was one thing he couldn't be, and that was optimistic. He held a knife to the throat of reality, and said, 'It's you or me,' whereupon it surrendered, and he crept into its belly and grew, and there was no telling whether it was pregnant with him or he with it.

Take colours, for instance. Has anyone ever heard of dewblue or bloodochre yellow, for instance? But Uncle Brock knew all about them and a great many other things besides, and the evening sky across the river over Remagen often reminds me of his rotting body and all the cheeky, snotty-nosed legends.

Then the evening turns into a cloak, and the ships approach, they're ugly, grey old women forgotten by death, women-ships, ship-women, with grinning, shrivelled, wrinkled faces and hair fluttering untidily on the mast. They drag their fat bellies along the stream-bed on bandy legs, and know nothing about the sky over Remagen, they waddle along between the broken bridges, and on board people sit and talk themselves hoarse and imagine there's a soul in their bodies. Nothing's so pure as a dirty mind.

There are some women who glow like radishes straight out of the garden, and when they walk they are like the dream of an engineer trying to compete with the latest Cadillac. Grutti is still as fresh as she was two years ago. She often says she has to take great care of herself, because relieving men of their surplus weight is a carefully calculated business. But the point is that she fits in with the Remagen sky, at any rate on many evenings, when the wind is favourable and comes from the north and you forget that it's a place for dying in.

I don't like this part of the world. I know about the smells and colours of the earth, and there are a lot of places where the wind catches you in the face like the fellow who shuts your eyes. I remember a place like it on the other side of Bobruisk, and the timber on the Beresina shrieked in the September

mist, fresh timber straight out of the forest, and
behind it there was a red cloud and the water was
purple, and the tree-trunks bled, and so did
Napoleon's troops. How cold is *simna, tovarishi?
Gospodin simna, tovarishi?* That's a sharp point on
the barrel in my belly and I don't like turning it, I
prefer drawing sap from my imagination, because
there goes religion prowling about on broad soles
and soft knees. Did I myself not see the elegant
musketeers in their gay, braided uniforms, and the
tough guards covered with medals and decorations
that were too heavy to float, so that the brave men
were borne down into the warm Beresina mud?
Come, brother, *Gospodin Simna*, Mr. Winter, is
cold, cold and evil and heartless.

So there are some things I have to guard against,
and then it's fine to be able to climb right outside
myself sometimes, get right away into the air for
hours and cross over on to the other side, and the
ding-dong in the belly I've left behind gets farther
and farther away and doesn't hurt or rasp, but
becomes painless, a spike with nothing to catch on,
a Grutti without clients.

What is a girl like Grutti? I'll tell you, because
when we crossed on the ferry – it was just about
two years ago now, and she was sitting on the seat
in the bows, and even before we spoke to her I had
squeezed the soul out of her body just as the wine-
growers here crush the juice out of their grapes,
and afterwards we spent three whole days here at
Remagen. I still plainly remember that morning,
the hard light on the Erpeler Ley, and the squalid
houses on the opposite bank, where the shadows

still played and the riverside road hung grey and
cool over the water.

It was the kind of morning when you feel like
laying your brow on the Rhine, staying quiet and
just feeling it. I don't like this part of the world,
but sometimes I go north or south, towards the
winter or the spring, and all the chugging ships
pass through my body and the fish swim through
my intestines, and I have to bend to pass under the
bridges, which smack their lips and whisper
quietly: Dewblue and bloodochre yellow, daybreak
seed and death in the deadly nightshade, and
Uncle Brock himself comes floating along, with
his laughter and his oaths, his yellow teeth and the
gaps between them, his strands of grey hair and
scraps of beard, and his death and burial in a small
rectangle of earth in the prison cemetery at Canndorf. We meet in the very middle of the Rhine,
half way between the two banks and the surface
and the bottom, and his pointed, faded bones go
straight into my barrel, and I play his song, about
the drinker and the ne'er-do-well, Jesus and Al
Capone, and Ali Baba without the forty thieves.
In the name of the seven tailed inquisition, the
story that has no beginning and no end begins on
the morning when we first saw Grutti on the ferry.

Grutti, I and the other two stayed in Remagen
for three days, and when the innkeepers told them
we had been there the day before and the day
before that and the day before that the ship's
crews in the taverns farted and were quite touched.
We glided imperceptibly from one day to the next,
and Grutti conjured them all up – Circe-Ger-

mania's big and little pigs, the reprobates that
sleep under bridges, the mulberry faces that
appear to little children in dreams, and on Grutti's
firm breasts they drummed out *God Save the King*
and the *Marseillaise* and finally a syncopated
version of the *Internationale* and bits of the Spanish
sky, and the song of Madrid the wonderful – ding-
dong, ding-dong – and Grutti ended by bursting
into tears, and so did the innkeepers and the
farting ship's crews and all of us, and only the
Rhine stayed dry and sober and went on carrying
its ships up to Basle and down to Rotterdam. But
I bet that he was only pretending to be so aloof, because with whom else could all those visions have
originated? Artless memories bearing the odours
of all the centuries through which he has flowed,
grey and unfathomable always, coming from a
beginning but going to no end, with us on his
banks. We are the coachmen in leather jerkins, and
the horsemen in the saddle of revenge pursuing the
enemy; or pursued by them, with fear at our backs,
beaten up, shot up, ravaged by syphilis, black
fever in our bodies, mouthing comforting blas-
phemies. Yes, we are myths the stream throws up
on its banks, and sometimes we think we see things
yawning at us, as if they knew they couldn't help
finding us boring. And sometimes we emerge
from the water in the form of shining, mute,
silvery fish, and then we die under the leaden sky
of Remagen in sight of the melancholy mountains.

Gone to the anglers.

When I looked at Grutti I said to myself: She's
a whore, and so must have been invented by

Hemingway. Only Hemingway's whores are so fresh and crystal clear and cold and built on slender, porcelain legs like skyscrapers of pleasure; and when they lie down they disclose a whole horizon of solid mountains and gentle hollows in which black bulls pasture and try to gore red rags and brave toreros . . . I was standing in front of the ferryboat and turned aside to look down the river towards holy Cologne and beyond it to busy but unholy Düsseldorf, where wallets full of crackling notes were waiting to be robbed, and excited, lascivious men sat gazing perplexedly in front of them, wondering where on earth Grutti was, Grutti, Grutti, Grutti, the magnificent hetaira, the woman from the east, Phallus Athene. If she were not a Hemingway whore, she must be a crazy one invented by William Faulkner, and in that case she could be expected to rise and climb up to the vineyards and fling herself down under the glassy sky, the sufferings of humanity turned into flesh. . . .

One should never say that mistakes have no influence on whatever it is one is mistaken about. Mistakes are what people do to us when they make use of us without giving any scope to our liberty. In Grutti's case you could plump for Hemingway or Faulkner, as you wished, but every choice has its consequences. But supposing Grutti was a *crazy* whore? As I walked down the gangway into the boat I remembered the angels dancing on the point of a needle. How many of them were there, and how much space was each one of them entitled to? Was it the same problem as on the Berlin underground on a week-end evening? And would there be room for the evening papers as well, including headlines, punctuation and horoscopes?

Actually I had been intending to go that morning to Cologne, where there was some money to be earned, because there was an incredibly decent Christian on Uncle Westdeutscher Rundfunk who was willing to give me printed paper notes in exchange for paper with my writing on it. But the journey down to Cologne is unattractive, the river soon turns away and the mountains vanish and the country loses its shape, and ends by smelling of shaken out dusters, unwashed handkerchiefs, and perfumed, sweaty feet. But I must get back to Uncle Brock, who must by now have had his mouth opened by the worms in his wooden box, oh, what a loud song there must be nine feet down below there where he now lives cheek by jowl with the foundation walls of Canndorf prison, you could almost reach him from the cellars if you could put your hand through the brick. He has been rotting for two years in his wooden box, on which they saved money by doing without paint, two years of mute song during which the barrel has been turning in my belly, ding-dong, ding-dong. You won't get me down, Uncle Brock sings, and the agony of the flesh is a lie, and heaven is a harp, and death grows a hand out of the wind; and the tune the wind plays on its harp is ding-dong, ding-dong-ding, and Uncle Brock rises out of the earth and stands in front of the prison walls and fiddles his tremendous tune to the white, fearful faces behind it. Prisoners arise, he proclaims, in the name of the rat-tailed, seven-headed inquisition, arise from your rotting coffins and sing to heaven, drowned men arise from the courses of the rivers in the name of the imperishable flesh and in view of the insatiable thirst of those who love and hate, you sons and daughters of the great wrath, the barrels have got new spikes, the great wrath is going about . . .

You ask who Uncle Brock was? He was my father's brother, a great paunch of a man in a black frock-coat. In my mind's eye I can still see him striding impressively through the streets, for in the pre-war period he was the lord of the town's dead. He had an undertaking business. Nowadays he would be described as the proprietor of a burial institution, but in those days undertaking was still just an ordinary business, and Uncle Brock was known to the whole town simply as Uncle Brock. He had a mouthful of golden teeth, and that made him look rather sinister, because in the sunshine, or under the lamps at night, fiery flashes shot out of his mouth.

My mother told me that he had had to make the dentist tipsy to get him to agree to filling his mouth with nothing but gold teeth. But what a set of teeth it was. A Rocky Mountains set, every tooth a *rocher de bronze*, and it was said that he could never open his lips or speak while at work, because if he had done so the dead would have risen again.

He was of course an unbeliever. My mother used to say that he didn't believe even in death, and that this was because he knew too much about it. But what happy times those were before the

war, when the interpreters of dreams still stewed
in their own juice and fanatics fattened themselves on turkeys. At that time my father had not
yet shot an American, and when the dead came
into Uncle Brock's hands they had a whole skin
and no holes in their skulls. What people died of in
our little town in those days? They died of con-
striction of the liver, or cancer, or bile, or obesity,
or phlegm, or women, or old age, and sometimes
of premonition, or the consequences of the previous
war, but all these things were accepted as familiar
and well attested by everyday life and experience,
and Uncle Brock, with those huge hands of his in
which a litre bottle could easily vanish, merely put
the full stop at the end of the sentence. But
honestly, who wouldn't die happy knowing that
afterwards Uncle Brock would be coming along
and pricking the bubble of the general embarrass-
ment with his cheerfulness? Life is not a game of
dice, and at the end of it there's nothing to be
gained that hasn't been gained beforehand.

Uncle Brock was married twice or three or four
times, no one knows for certain, he couldn't be sure
himself, and right to the end of the war our
register office was burnt out, and the registrar was
so completely carbonised that he gave Uncle Brock
a lot of trouble. My mother says that by the end of
the war he had grown quite silent, and only those
who know how talkative the old rogue normally
was can appreciate what that meant. But men
change in the course of their lives, they get thin or
fat, quiet or gluttonous, they're sometimes stupid
and sometimes clever, and Uncle Brock ended by

weighing no more than seven stone, and people no longer trusted him across the street. But when they were dead it was too late, and when he came into the house to deal with them and take them away there was nothing they could do about it.

Of course people started talking long beforehand, and it was just as well that when it got into the papers he was safely under arrest and no longer able to walk the streets, because they were so angry that they easily might have lynched him. For a time they even forgot that there was no one else in the town who could deal with the dead so well and efficiently. But a man who helps himself to gold fillings from the mouths of the dead can't help rousing resentment, and it made no difference that everyone knew that uncle for a long time had had a kink about gold teeth. Whenever one of his women – whether he had just married her or was merely living with her – had the toothache he always bribed the dentist to extract the tooth and replace it with a gold one. Uncle Brock was a worthy citizen, and when he walked through the streets he inspired respect, respect of death, and people forgave him a great deal, such as his occasional disappearances for a few days at a time – in winter these were actually rather frequent. Anyone who died during those absences of his had to await burial until his return. It was only after the war, when he vanished for a time and then came back without any teeth, and also that other matter became generally known, that he was temporarily unpopular. Afterwards, when he was sent to prison and died there, the resentment was forgotten, and I'm sure they've gone back to telling stories in the taverns about the old boozer Brock and the way he handled women and corpses, and I should give a great deal to be able to go and listen to them, but here I am stranded far away under the twilight sky of Remagen, where my father shot an American. I know this from Uncle Brock himself, because father never told any of us, neither my mother nor my brother nor me; he confided it only to his brother. By that time he was no longer quite here but was already half way over, and after the funeral Uncle Brock went off again for the last time in his life, because soon after he came back he was locked up. He came westwards to this precise spot, because father told him every detail. He came here to Remagen, and to Erpel and Kasbach on the other side of the river, and he talked to people, and they corroborated everything father had said. When he came back he was quite different, and he said to me: 'Young man, your father killed an American.' When he said this to me in that changed manner of his the barrel in my belly suddenly started turning furiously, and it wasn't spikes, but knives and bayonets that made the music. Then mother came in. 'Good heavens, Johann, where have you left your teeth?' she exclaimed. That made me realise why he looked so different, and why his face had fallen in so and looked so shrivelled under his hat. He hadn't a tooth left in his head, and he said it had been a bad but necessary bit of business. This made my mother furious, women always jump to con-

clusions, but all Uncle Brock said was: 'Sergeant
Henry Terduzzi.'

My mother fell silent, as if she had been
thunderstruck. The story behind it was this.
Throughout the war my father had served at home
in the Landwehr, and it wasn't till the very end
that he was sent to the front, which then ran along
the Rhine, and in the freshly raked vineyards one
cloudy afternoon two men fired at each other, and
one of them was the Italian American Henry
Terduzzi and the other was my father, who had not
had to fire a single shot in anger throughout the
war, and the ill-starred Italian American lay still
and didn't move again. 'Now are you angry with
me because of my teeth?' Uncle Brock shouted.
'They're crossing the big pond, just like Henry
Terduzzi's body did.' Uncle Brock explained that,
as he had no money left, he had had to sell his
teeth, his own teeth, because the dead man's
parents were poor and had to be sent something.

What were we to say to that? Mother grumbled
for a bit, and then went into the kitchen and lit the
oven.

A fortnight later Uncle Brock was arrested for
desecrating the dead.

By the time I got round to the idea of counting
the years since Swift's death we had spent three
days on our Remagen pub-crawl, searching all the
time for the mythology of the Rhine. Henry
Terduzzi was dead as irrevocably as Swift and
Gogol and Grimmelshausen. Why do new books
go on being written? We sat by the riverside in the
evening light, and tinfoil wrappings glittered among

the freshly polished broken glass, we were surrounded by the gladness of a high summer day, and fat families from Germany and dried up looking families from England and perspiring Dutchwomen looking for their husbands gathered on the riverside promenade, and the wooden cross on the top of the Erpeler Ley overhung everything and stared down uncomprehendingly. We spent a long time at old Kriebe's place, the Lucullus. When fat Marie put the beer on our table she looked indignantly at Grutti's outstretched, stockingless legs – Holy Mother of God, how sinful you tippling whores of Babylon are. Fat Marie, who smelt of shoe polish and was muffled in six yards of sweaty material, hurried off to serve other guests, and old Kriebe, surrounded by bottles and glasses and piles of notes, trumpeted away behind the counter like a laughing great elephant. He had spent many years at sea, and his tavern was full of stuffed fish and wooden models of steamers and sailing ships, it was both saloon and ocean and primeval forest, jungle and sea-bed, with dark secrets and sharp smells, stained tablecloths, subdued lights and the wry faces of solitary drinkers. As it was summer, they had hired an old fashioned band, consisting of three middle-aged fellows with red noses and heavy hands. Twice a week Schott, the travel guide, unloaded his pleasure-seeking Dutch tourists into the tavern in the evening, and they drank watered wine and adulterated *Schnapps*, and the band strummed out polkas and Rhenish dances, and the Dutchmen seized their shiny-faced women and stamped

round in their heavy shoes and sang *Warchum
istis am Rhain so chöön.* Later we were left to ourselves. Schott took his perspiring charges off to bed
and came back, this time with an open, naked face
without his spectacles, a human being among other
human beings, fat Marie went off to say her
prayers, old Kriebe brought some decent bottles to
the table, and Brutti blew so much smoke into the
faces of the band that their three red noses looked
as if they were on fire. Oh, you night-time ogres
and devils, sometimes I'm afraid Grutti is only a
dream, and the nights are a pulp that I cut with my
pocket knife, but under the blade they turn into
the head of Sergeant Henry Terduzzi, whom my
father killed, and then Grutti is nothing but a doll
made of paper and paste with strings attached to
her arms and legs, and her enormous eyelids open
and shut because someone pulls the strings.
Eventually I went to the station and bought myself a ticket to Cologne, and the man at the booking
office had a swollen face, as if he had just taken a
terrible beating up in the boxing ring. When he
gave me my change he asked me through his glass
window whether I wasn't so-and-so who wrote
books. So it had already come out, and people were
talking. Then he said something silly about Goethe,
and I remembered there was something else I
wanted to ask Grutti, because human beings cannot help questioning the souls out of each other's
bodies. 'Do you happen to have an old pair of
gloves here?' I asked the man after pocketing my
change. He shook his head sorrowfully, and I
made off. In any case he wouldn't have understood

why I wanted a pair of old gloves that morning under the Remagen sun that was just climbing over the mountains. There are some mornings when you want to hide in the dark security of a glove, to grope your way blindly about the day, unable to see, unable to think, unable to hear – the barrel in my belly was turning angrily and painfully, as if a rat had been let loose in my intestines – ding-dong, ding-dong, those were no points, they were teeth, sharp teeth tearing my flesh from the inside, but what they didn't know and what helped me was the trick of getting out of myself, because I didn't want to meet my Henry Terduzzi. What did Don Quixote die of? He was trampled to death by a lot of drunken, grunting pigs. Why didn't you slaughter pigs instead of charging windmills, you old fool? But that's fate, it sends one man pigs and another an Italian *ersatz* American, but for me the Rhine washed Grutti ashore, and so we lay among the stones and rusty tin cans under the reproachful overcast sky of Remagen, four extinct volcanoes, four craters with a hoarse death rattle in our throats, issuing no more smoke and with bloodshot eyes, parched throats longing for fresh spittle, stranded in the desert between Vladivostok and Gibraltar, caught in the spider's web of the universe. Then the movement started up again in my belly, the barrel turned, ding-dong, ding-dong; and moreover I hereby bequeath to the hospital as raw material for bandages all the spider's webs that are stuck to the windows of heaven here. . . . That was a song that came out of the river and the rusty tin cans, descended from the mountains and

arose out of the ground, and came out of my throat
– dewblue and bloodochre yellow, daybreak seed
and death in the deadly nightshade, and Uncle
Brock came floating along, with his oaths and his
laughter, his strands of hair and scraps of beard and
all the strange dreams that haunt us – we haunt
ourselves, and the permanent guests of the Great
Drift danced together, and memory came down
firmly over the blown up bridge of Remagen, a
paper carriageway, a dream over the depths, and
then the white-painted stone is a reminder of the
men who went crashing down to the fishes with the
bridge to where no moonlight reaches and the
glassy sky of Remagen smiles no more. 'Yes, I
knew him,' Grutti said. That made me realise why
I had recognised her, I had seen her on the ferry
with his eyes, Uncle Brock's eyes. That's the way
things happen, you walk blindly down the street
and suddenly you see someone you know. I know
the men in the river very well, even though all I
can see is the painted cross on the wreckage. I
know Sergeant Henry Terduzzi, and I can see his
body swimming the big pond. Every July Grutti
comes here for three days. She promised Uncle
Brock to send money to Terduzzi's mother and
father, and she says she does so, but I know she
doesn't, because at heart she's mean, she helped
Uncle Brock to drink the money he got from his
set of teeth, though she had no need to. But she
met him here at that time, and he took her to the
place in the vineyard where my father shot Terduzzi. There's also something else I know about
Grutti that no one else knows. Uncle Brock had

with him a leather bag full of gold teeth, and they sold them and sent the money to America. 'As if the Americans weren't rich enough already,' Grutti still says indignantly. But Uncle Brock was not to be diverted, and, though he was going downhill rapidly, he had his way, as he always did when he had set his heart on something. He said that our dead who died at home could perfectly well go to heaven or (where he believed they were going) hell without any gold teeth in their mouths. This wasn't vengeance, but retributive justice as between one people and another, he explained to Grutti. When the tall, blond young men at Auschwitz played the dentist and searched for Jewish gold with forceps, these people had dutifully kept their mouths shut and looked the other way, and now that they were dead they could at least do something to square accounts, particularly as it didn't hurt anyone. It had hurt those others at the time.

When Grutti heard this she didn't dare say anything, though she regretted the money, and couldn't see why he had to send it to America of all places. I explained that he had a kink about gold teeth. 'Oh, yes, I know,' she said, 'and when he had no money left we sold his own set of teeth. And how is the old chap now?' This made me realise that she didn't know. Perhaps I ought to have told her he was dead, but instead I said he was very well, and his business was doing fine, it was like hers, it always did well, both always survived everything. That made her laugh, and I raised my nonexistent hat to my dead Uncle Brock, whom

Grutti still hoped to meet here, because he still
haunted her memory and made her come here
every year to the local dives and the vineyards and
the rusty ferry-boat under the strangely crooked
Remagen sky.

At this point I ought to come clean and say
straight out whether Grutti was a Hemingway
whore or a crazy William Faulkner one, but I
prefer to assume that either would be an unjustified
translation from the American.

Who is Grutti, then? I'll tell you. She's Hemingway and William Faulkner, Ben Hur and
Cervantes, Christ and Lucifer, a white mouse and
Chinese pride in fertility, an Eskimo and Joseph
Kainz, whipped cream and coitus, a machine-gun
and Zanzibar, a freshly painted and decorated
Irish church, and a sixteenth-century Central
Rhineland house of pleasure. I live on the Rhine,
but my home-town is east of it, nine feet deep in
the earth, and its name is Uncle Brock, and it has a
main street along which we all have to pass,
whether today or tomorrow or even yesterday, for
it is paved with our bones and the cries of horror and
the songs of all the angels and devils that men
have been, are, will be, have not been, are not and
never will be. How many years has Swift been
dead? He won't die till tomorrow, and besides, he
never existed, any more than Shakespeare did, if
you disregard the fact that the man who actually
wrote his plays was someone of the same name.
When we pushed off on our way over to Remagen
the ferryman tried to persuade me that Grutti was
not quite right in the head. He said she came here

at the same time every year and wandered about
the vineyards. Every year at the same time a sort of
fit came over her, she grew restive, and sometimes
spent the whole day on the ferry, not eating or
drinking but just staring straight ahead and sometimes waving in the direction of the Ley. 'I tell you
she's not quite right in the head,' the ferryman
said. 'But she's got money, thank heaven, she can
pay.'

'Please show this man off my boat, officer,' the
ferryman said. 'It's the same thing every year, he
comes here and wants to spend the whole day
going backwards and forwards, but he hasn't any
money.' 'Come along, be reasonable, come ashore,'
said the policeman. 'He says his name's Grutti,'
said the ferryman. 'Normally he's perfectly all
right, but once a year it comes over him and he
says his name's Grutti.' 'You impertinent devil,'
I said, 'you know Grutti just as well as I do, you
earn enough out of her and her story, you've got
your eyes on her, you dirty old fat drunken pig.'
'It's the same thing every year,' the ferryman said
to the policeman, 'it comes over him every year like
this, his father killed an American up there, and he
can't get it out of his mind, and also he seems to
have had an uncle who wasn't quite right either.'
They took me back to the Erpel side and put me
ashore. I really meant to go to holy Cologne, where
I know a delightful character named Stiegenwein
who works on the radio there and sometimes gives
me printed bank-notes in exchange for paper
covered with my scribble, but this time I didn't

go, because I didn't want to leave from here, I
wanted to leave from Remagen on the other side,
so I came back. I can't stand the right bank here,
the air's too dry, because the whole country insists
on it with all the boring proofs of its reality. You
can dream only on the other side, under the
crystal sky of Remagen. One day I shall find that
printed in a big book, and it will be the only
sentence in it printed without losing credibility in
the process. What is life? It's a gullet, a throat for
drinking. What is death? A slit gullet, a putrifying
Uncle Brock, a dream of Grutti, a bit of madness
that no one has tasted to the full. Ding-dong goes
the barrel in my belly, and that's the signal for me
to get out of myself and mount into the crystal
clear sky over Remagen and descend into the timelessness of the river, for the ships to sail through
my belly and for the fish to swim about inside me.
What a marvellous aquarium is man.

SULZER

How I got to Kaff Kutzbach? It was through Sulzer, Ernest Sulzer, the man's not as American as his name. I met him at Berlin Free Radio, where he was the Eastern Political Department, *was* the Eastern Political Department, because his name was a programme and he was a party in himself, his voice was a division that smashed into the enemy's lines, mopped up his trenches, broke up his position, demoralised his troops ideologically and gave them the political and moral knock-out.

That is the kind of person Sulzer was, and he took me under his wing and managed me a bit when I turned up there. He always had a cigarette in the corner of his mouth, and his hat was always askew on his grey, bristly head, the collar of his overcoat was always turned up, and the clever eyes behind those rimless gold spectacles of his looked at you penetratingly and sceptically. To judge by his exterior, he might have walked straight out of an American film, so exactly was he modelled on them; he was, in fact, a duplicate of the Statue of Liberty that had been signed on by the Central Intelligence Agency and disguised as Mr. X.

He stuffed a ticket into my overcoat pocket with a good-natured grin, and I took off from Tempelhof airport and flew over the split mushroom of Germany, and when we landed at Wahn for Cologne I heaved a sigh of relief. At Cologne I spent a week listening to what the well endowed experts on eastern Europe had to say, and on Saturday, when we were all thoroughly tired of the Eastern European Institute, Sulzer appeared in

person with the inevitable cigarette in the corner
of his mouth, his hat askew on the grey stubble of
his head, and his overcoat collar turned up. He
strode to the rostrum, divested himself of his overcoat and hat, put his cigarette down somewhere, the
good-natured eyes behind his spectacles twinkled
at us cheerfully, and he began pitching into the
Communists and singing the praises of liberty in a
way that deprived us of sight and hearing. He
spoke without pausing for breath, in fact he didn't
pause at all, he bombarded us with technical
expressions, exaggerations, acute points, the
results of secret service work, lay philosophy,
humanistic tit-bits, Communist theories, American
slang. He didn't so much make a speech as give a
performance that took away our breath, carried us
off, ravished and enraptured us. He spread jam
behind our ears and rammed ideology down our
throats, and he talked like a sprinter who had
strayed into a marathon race and was clocking up
the miles at a hundred-yards pace because it
seemed too stupid to admit he had made a mistake.

He talked and talked, and the end of his speech
was totally lost, because no one could possibly take
it in, it was simply drowned in an outburst of en-
thusiasm that broke down all barriers and carried
everything before it, causing us to shout and clap
and the scales to fall from our eyes and see the
plain and obvious truth, namely that powerful and
gigantic Russia was neither powerful nor gigantic.
We saw everything through the sharp eyes of Mr.
Dulles and realised how blind we had been. We
had had revealed to us what held the world

together in its innermost parts and how it could be
taken to pieces – the Russian, Communist world,
that is to say, because that was the world he was
talking about.

'Was I good?' Sulzer, master of understatement,
asked afterwards as we rattled along in the train
from Cologne on the Rhine to Linz on the Rhine.
'Was I good?' Cologne, Porz, Troisdorf, Beuel,
Ober-Kassel, Königswinter, Honnef, Unkel, Erpel,
Linz – the train went on and stopped and went on
again, and people got out and others got in, and I
was given the speech all over again for my private
benefit, and he was as good in private as he was in
public, he was a decent fellow and he was convinc-
ing.

At Linz he walked quickly through the barrier
with contracted eyes, turned sharp left, stopped at
the kiosk and bought a dozen newspapers, the
names of which I prefer not to mention to avoid
giving them a free advertisement. Sulzer read all
the important papers. We walked from Linz to
Kutzbach, though there's a bus, but we preferred
walking. You follow the railway line on the left-
hand side, turn left to the road, follow it for two
hundred yards, and from there you can either take
the main road to the Kutzbach underpass, where
the traffic is regulated by a gentleman swinging a
wooden leg, or you can take the next underpass to
the right along a narrow path that runs along the
railway embankment on the Rhine side. We chose
the latter. Sulzer walked ahead reading the paper,
and I followed behind, carrying his suitcase, and
that was how I arrived at Kaff Kutzbach on a

winter Saturday. The weather was foul. There was
no wind, but no snow either, there were only a few
dirty white patches on the mountain-tops though it
was January, but winter lagged everywhere that
year, and here in the Rhine valley there were only a
few brief spells of frost at night, and in the daytime
the thermometer was three or four degrees above
freezing point. Sulzer read his dozen newspapers,
and he simply dropped those that didn't interest
him, so our way from Linz to Kaff Kutzbach was
marked as if we were taking part in a paper-chase.
But who was the hare and who were the hounds?
And that was how we reached the doctor's.

When you get to the place by the path we took
you first pass some villas and then you go under the
railway line into the village, and that's where the
doctor lives in one of the little houses on the left.
He's a big man with a magnificent head, slowly
getting thin on top, with bushy eyebrows, a handsome chin and fine hands. He is a reassuring person
to meet, for he instantly inspires and radiates
confidence, though the conditions in which he was
living were in the most violent possible contrast
with everything any ordinary person would expect
of a doctor.

We knocked, and he called out, 'Come in,' and
there he was standing in his kitchen/living room in
the midst of the most indescribable chaos.

Sulzer had, of course, prepared me for what to
expect, and in any case I had passed the stage at
which one shows astonishment openly. I prided
myself on knowing something about the world, and
I knew that one should preserve a calm exterior and

take everything as a matter of course. So I stumbled
in Sulzer's wake into the dark and musty room.
Eventually I inferred the existence of a sink,
chiefly from the presence over it of a blackened
pipe with a tap sticking out from the wall. All
round it, in it, and under it there was a pile of dirty
crockery, a whole mountain of crockery, and someone had skilfully made a passage-way through it,
so skilfully that the mountain, defying all the laws
of statics, miraculously failed to collapse. In the
middle of the passage-way there was a solitary
aluminium saucepan, and I eventually discovered
that it was used for all purposes, including making
coffee, cooking, and washing up, in so far as the
latter was absolutely necessary and the dirty crocks
could not be left lying about. When we arrived the
doctor, who was in a torn shirt and patched old
trousers, was shaving, using a fragment of broken
mirror attached to the wall by means of two nails
and a bit of wire, and he was dipping his shaving
stick in the aluminium saucepan.

When he saw us he screwed his great foam-
covered face into a grimace and said:

'For God's sake shut the door – and don't move,
or the house will fall in.'

We stopped in our tracks. Sulzer froze into an
American pillar of salt with his hand held out in
greeting. I hardly dared breathe.

The doctor threw away his shaving stick, raised
his head, gazed at the ceiling and said:

'The slightest movement and the whole house
will blow up. Minute differences, such as the
variations in nuance of the same thought in two

different minds, the divergence of impact made on two observers by the same picture, provide the amoeba-like foundation on which world revolution is based.'

Sulzer burst out laughing. The doctor laughed, too, and his voice mounted to a falsetto. I was astonished that such a huge frame could produce a schoolgirl giggle. Meanwhile he had stopped shaving. He wiped the lather from his face on a bit of rag which had presumably once been a towel, and with a wealth of courteous phrases and gestures invited us to be seated, which was more easily said than done, because the room was so cluttered that it was possible neither to stand nor sit comfortably.

I looked round.

The old wallpaper was scarcely visible because of the newspapers and books piled along the walls, and the table and three chairs were loaded with printed matter, too. In between the piles were cooking utensils and glasses and articles of clothing, as well as pictures and other things it was impossible to identify without holding them up to the light. We cleared two chairs, and with some difficulty the doctor made room for himself on the creaking sofa.

'Have you any news from Vorkuta?' Sulzer asked.

The doctor shook his head anxiously.

'No,' he said. 'But they really seem to be doing away with the camp. Strunk was here last week, and he thinks so, too. I've had a letter from Ott, he's proposing to stay on in Tokyo, to track down the old Gestapo network. He believes it still to be

pretty well intact, the Japanese never really
cracked it, and then the Americans stepped in, and
so the old Nazis started working for them straight
away. Oh, I completely forgot to tell you, Heidi has
got out. She spent the last six months in the Lub-
yanka, and now has made contact with Junkers in
west Berlin, and she says she wants to drop in
here next week. You might go and see her when
you get back, she's said to be in a pretty bad way,
the after-effects of prison.' The doctor ended his
speech with a long expletive in Russian.

Sulzer produced a snow-white handkerchief and
blew his nose immoderately loudly. He folded the
handkerchief again, carefully stuffed it into the
pocket of his faultless, grey, made-to-measure suit,
but realised that he hadn't finished yet, produced
the handkerchief again, and blew his nose loudly
all over again. When he had finished his eyes were
red and tears were rolling down his cheeks.

'Your revolution has gone to the devil,' he said
with an expression of the deepest satisfaction.
Then he dropped his voice, and added: 'When one
considers how it began, one can almost regret it.
Think of the heights it reached with Lenin and
Trotsky, and then this bank robber, this Vissari-
onovich from the backwoods, from Russian
Turkey, who can think of nothing better than
cutting poor muzhiks' throats. The more I think
about it, the more plainly I see that we, the ex-
Communists, are the only revolutionaries left.'

He looked at me with his red-rimmed eyes,
seeking for my agreement. I had no views on the
matter one way or the other, but somehow I liked

the idea. Wasn't it Koestler who said that the last
battle would be between Communists and ex-
Communists? Or, if it wasn't Koestler, was it
Silone? Or if it wasn't Ignazio could it have been –
but there are many saints in the ex-Communist
calendar.

The doctor laid his fine hands on the table and
contemplated them, palm upwards, and he looked
as if he were reading them when he said:

'Why on earth didn't the Americans intervene in
1953? And why did they stand idle in 1956 when
things blew up in Hungary? Mistakes like that are
simply incomprehensible. If a single armoured
division had been put in, revolt would have flared
through the people's democracies, eastern Germany and the Soviet Union itself.'

'Dulles stands alone,' Sulzer answered, hoarse
with anger. 'He lacks good collaborators. We need
a hundred, a thousand men like Dulles. Eisen-
hower has a box of fleas in his head, if Dulles were
President . . .'

'Can't you whisper that to your friends in
Washington?' the doctor asked.

Sulzer had been chain-smoking ever since our
arrival. He didn't wait to finish one cigarette before
opening his gold cigarette case, taking out another
with trembling fingers, lighting it, and flinging its
only half-smoked predecessor in the direction of
the sink.

The doctor rose, emptied the shaving water
from the aluminium saucepan, filled it with fresh
water, and put it on the wobbly fireplace. The fire
was blazing, and when the water had boiled we all

started looking for the tea, and eventually it was
found. We waited for some time, cleaned three
glasses and poured it out. Sulzer produced a bottle
of vodka from his suitcase and topped up the tea
with it and, though what we drank was fifty-fifty
tea and vodka, I thought I could detect a distinct
taste of soap from the doctor's shaving water.

I didn't dare remark on this, but when Sulzer
started sipping the doctor nodded to him and said:

'Tastes of soap, doesn't it?'

'In the camp it often used to.'

That put things on the right track.

'What became of *makhorka* Joe?'

The tea with vodka and soap had a stimulating
effect and put spice into the afternoon. The doctor
produced some strong Rhenish black bread and
pickles, and we fell to. Afterwards Sulzer relapsed
into gloomy silence, but the doctor made up for it
by holding forth at length, as often happens with
people who live alone a great deal and are inclined
to brood. I waited for a pause in the flow and said:

'Do you live alone here?'

'No, I don't live here at all, this is my mother's
house,' the doctor said. 'She's seventy, and in
hospital with a cavity the size of a fist in her left
lung, and I'm afraid she won't come back. When
I went to see her last week she was nothing but skin
and bone, and I think it can be only a question of
days.'

He nodded his head sadly, and there was a dull
gleam in his eyes, the colour of which was not
discernible in the darkness of the room. Sulzer sat
in silence, breathing out vast amounts of cigarette

smoke. So this is the west German left, I said to myself, the ex-Communists, the anti-Communists, the disillusioned of yesterday and today, fading away in embittered isolation, acute analysts without power, revolutionaries of the soul who conceal their soul and enrich their faces with sceptical wrinkles.

'How long have you been living here, doctor?' I asked.

'Six months.'

'And where did you live before?'

'Oh, here, there, and everywhere, a furnished room is good enough for me. I'm an undemanding person.'

'And why did you give up your practice?'

He didn't like this question. He laughed, and his big, fleshy, handsome face was full of uncertainty. The fine fingers of his fine hands quivered and he put his right hand through his open shirt and laid it on the mass of curly black hair on his chest, where the fingers moved uncertainly.

'Why did you give it up? Tell me,' I repeated.

Sulzer intervened.

'Read Dostoievsky, and you'll understand everything,' he said.

The doctor nodded his head in relief.

'What has Dostoievsky to do with it?' I asked.

A trace of anger was discernible in the doctor's face. He pointed at Sulzer sitting in his cloud of smoke and said:

'He has been writing a book about Dostoievsky for twenty years.'

This revelation took me aback. I was prepared

for anything, but the idea of my classical, super-American Sulzer sitting at his desk writing a book about Dostoievsky I found really extraordinary. It struck me as phoney, reminded me of war films in which the hero before, between and after battles in enemy country enters a church still standing in the midst of the general devastation and sits down and plays the organ. I said nothing of this, as in the first place I lacked the courage, and in the second I had not for a long time been certain enough of my own beliefs and feelings to expose them to the ordeal of open discussion.

But the doctor cleared up the situation.

'He,' he said, pointing to Sulzer, 'is the son of a Mecklenburg farm-hand. Do you know what that means?'

'I can imagine it.'

'Good. Do you know the Count of Koteletto?'

'If you mean the east Berlin radio commentator, of course I do. He's as famous as a calf with two heads,' I said.

'Gavrilovich, now hold your breath,' the doctor went on. 'The Count of Koteletto is the son of the Mecklenburg landowner for whom Sulzer's father worked.'

I didn't hold my breath, though I saw the point. The farm-hand's son as anti-Communist spokesman on the west Berlin radio, and the noble landowner's son as spokesman on the other side.

I looked at the infant prodigy Sulzer, and a thought came into my mind that I tried to chase away, but it kept coming back. Then I blurted it out.

'And what did he do in Hitler's time?'

I pointed at Sulzer, as the doctor liked doing.

Sulzer leapt to his feet as if he had been kicked in the behind and brandished his fists in my face, looking at me furiously with his short-sighted, red-rimmed eyes.

'If I've touched a painful nerve, my name's Joseph,' I said.

'There's no need to call yourself Joseph, it wouldn't suit you anyway,' the doctor said soothingly. 'But you've got the wrong end of the stick.'

Sulzer calmed down as suddenly as he had flared up. He took out his gold cigarette case, helped himself to a cigarette with trembling fingers, lit it, and put it in his mouth the wrong way round, with the burning end between his lips.

Strangely enough, this seemed to make practically no difference to him. He sullenly closed the incident in a cloud of smoke.

'During the Nazi period Sulzer was a street-sweeper in Berlin,' the doctor said quietly.

Sulzer was not mentioned again until the evening, and he took no part in the talk, but remained stubbornly silent, drinking vodka and blowing his nose.

Everything the doctor talked about quickly faded from my mind, for one thing because there was such a lot of it and for another because all those speeches about freedom at the symposium on eastern Europe at Cologne had got me down. But there was an exception. One of his stories implanted itself so firmly in my mind that I could still repeat it almost word for word. He told it to me while he was talking his experiences in the Russian penal camp at Vorkuta. I no longer remember how it happened, but we got round to military matters, and that brought us to the behaviour of senior officers.

The doctor said that before his time as a camp inmate he had only once in his life met a general in flesh and blood. Then he was suddenly confronted with thirty generals all at once. They occupied the plank beds on the left side of the hut and his was on the right. 'I watched them and listened to their conversation,' he said. 'It was an eerie experience. They addressed each other in the third person, incorporating the rank of the individual addressed on each occasion. They did this first thing in the morning when they inquired of each other how they had slept, and over their tea when they offered each other the sugar. The commandant ended by forbidding them to call each other *Herr General*, but in vain; they went on using their generals' jargon. Addressing each other in the third person was the corset of their souls, and the faded gold braid on their hats was its substance. War memories filled their day, and their favourite subject was the *Blitzkrieg* as waged in Poland and France. Post-1943 memories were repressed, and they spoke of the capitulation with manly grief. The horizon of their conversation was bounded by the walls of Prussian barrack yards.

'Since the war the question has often been asked how the German army was able to tolerate a hysteric and neuropath as supreme commander, and the answer was facing me in my hut, drinking

warm water with a bit of sugar. Hitler's war gave
these generals their chance. Without him they
would have remained what they were – captains
or majors with no prospect of obtaining in decades
the positions to which they rose in a few years of
war. Without them he would never have been able
to play his lunatic military game.'

The lowest point of Kaff Kutzbach is at Rhine
level. You leave the busy highroad, go under the
railway bridge, and when you reach the first houses
and the transport company car park you have got a
hundred yards further, but no higher. Flood water
sometimes reaches this spot, but just beyond the
first turning, shortly before the church, the
asphalted village street begins to wind uphill,
narrowing all the way. The last and highest
building, five minutes walk from the end of the
village, is a tavern called the Green Lamp, and the
doctor took Sulzer and me there on the evening of
our arrival, because there was going to be a meeting. We were the first to arrive, Sulzer still
taciturn, the doctor still cheerfully and excitedly
talking away, and I with a big note-book in my
coat-pocket in which I proposed surreptitiously to
make notes from time to time. We waited for the
people to turn up, and gradually they did so. There
was Count Pertinax with his latest girl-friend, the
dark and highly made up daughter of a saw-mill
owner from the Eifel; Hanz Zauder, former editor
of the east Berlin *Woche;* Karla Sternbann, an
unmarried woman who had taught Chinese at the
Socialist Union Party school; Rudolfs, a teacher

from Dresden who must have been in his fifties
and had served as a general in the jungle in North
Vietnam under Ho Chi-minh and now lived with
a girl of twenty-one named Sonja who had not
completed her German studies at Dresden Univer-
sity; Natasha Bielinsky-Kastun, who wrote for the
principal newspapers and enjoyed especial esteem
in the Kutzbach circle because her father had been
one of Lenin's closest associates and the great man
was said to have lifted her out of her cradle and
kissed her on the cheek soon after she was born;
Mr. Bill MacGriffe, a full-cheeked, highly intel-
lectual product of the Massachusetts Institute of
Technology and probably also a high-up in the
American secret service – he later became one of
Kennedy's advisers; and Professor Herbert Weber,
a historian with a phenomenal memory who could
tell you the name of anybody who had ever been a
member of the central committee of any of the
world's Communist parties, and when. But the
greatest attraction did not turn up till nearly ten
o'clock, when he arrived straight from Cologne.
He was awaited with special interest and greeted
with acclamation, and was no other than Volodya
Leonardov, well known throughout the country
because of his books and television appearances,
an amiable little man who suffered because of his
small stature, because he had to look up at everyone. His special distinguishing marks were his
upswept hair, his laugh, which developed into a
breathless giggle, and the extraordinarily beautiful
but mute young woman by whom he was accom-
panied. She turned out to be his latest acquisition.

She was Italian and could speak hardly a word of German, and the friendly silence which she therefore preserved was another thing that produced a wave of sympathy.

The doctor took me aside. 'What keeps you in west Berlin?' he asked. 'Why don't you come here, where you would be among friends?' And he went on talking for some time.

'But where should I live?' I asked. He said that could be arranged. For the time being there was a lovely summer-house in the middle of a rose garden with a view over the Rhine that I could use.

I thought it over. Why not, after all? In west Berlin one was too near east Berlin. Why not get away from it for a time?

He asked me what my plans were, and I told him I wanted to write.

'Have you ambitions?' he asked.

I didn't understand.

'Literary ambitions,' he explained. 'Do you want to write literature?'

'Oh, literature,' I said. 'In these times one should merely register things.'

'And what's hindering you?'

'That's just the point.'

'But what is hindering you?'

'I'm hindering myself,' I said.

'Very well,' he said. 'Move to our summer-house on the Rhine, you won't find a spot as beautiful and rewarding anywhere else in Germany.'

He looked at me penetratingly.

'With one exception,' I said.

'Exception?' he exclaimed. 'What exception?'

'There's one other beautiful and rewarding spot in Germany, and it's the Elbe, the sandstone mountains of the Elbe.'

'Good heavens alive!' he exclaimed, roaring with laughter. 'Good heavens alive, man, so far as you're concerned that now lies in the depths of Siberia.'

'Yes,' I said quietly, 'yes, for me that now lies in the depths of Siberia.'

Sulzer and I walked back from Kutzbach by the path along the railway line by which we had come. From Linz Sulzer took the train to Frankfurt, where his next audience was awaiting him. I took the train to Beuel, from where I went by tram to Bonn, took the airline bus to the airport and flew back to Berlin, thinking about Kaff Kutzbach.

Sulzer and I spent two nights there in the bedroom over the doctor's living-room/kitchen. The doctor slept on the creaking sofa in the kitchen, he said that in any case he never used his parents' bedroom, so we slept under the thick feather-bedding on the double-bed. Old-fashioned, yellowing, pathetically absurd portraits looked down at us from the wall. The Rhine splashed past and trains thundered past, and in the middle of the night Sulzer started talking, and this woke me up. He had sat up and was leaning forward in the bed, and he went on talking, and I listened to him repeating word for word his speech about the Communist menace. 'I was a Communist myself,' he said, 'I was a friend of Johannes R. Becher's, in

1927 I was expelled from the party, and I know
what Communism means,' he said, and he paused
at all the right places, the places where we had
applauded. I got up and switched on the light, but
he was not to be diverted, and he went on talking
with his eyes half open, looking naked without his
rimless gold spectacles, gazing at the feather bed
as if he were facing an audience, his face motionless
and only his lips moving. I switched off the light
again, crept back into bed, pulled the bedding over
my ears, and listened to him making his speech in
his sleep, making me his speech in his sleep, and
next morning he knew nothing whatever about it.
But he knew he was beginning to talk in his sleep
and wanted to know what he said.

When we shook hands on the platform at Linz
he looked me in the eye.

'You're a cold fish,' he said, with the greatest
friendliness and the assured experience of an older
man. 'You shouldn't just confine yourself to coldly
registering things,' he said. 'I had a peep at your
notebook, you're a regular filing cabinet. But that's
not enough, man has a soul. Read Dostoievsky.'

At that he pressed my hand firmly and got into
the train.

I wanted to answer him. I wanted to tell him
how wrong he was, I wanted to tell him that there
were times when you should restrict yourself to
coldly recording things, otherwise you just got
carried off into the dark realms of the fantastic. I
wanted to tell him that if I left Berlin and came to
Kutzbach it would be to escape from the grimace
of the fantastic and to search for empirical truths.

But Sulzer was on the way to Frankfurt, where his next audience was awaiting him.

I took the train to Beuel, and from there I went by tram to Bonn and took the airline bus to Wahn airport. Have I mentioned that already? Well, it's perfectly true, but I didn't do so immediately. First I went back again to Kutzbach.

The doctor was lying on the sofa, fast asleep in the midst of the indescribable confusion.

I awakened him.

'What happened last night?' I asked.

'Ye gods, were we drunk,' the doctor groaned. 'Only death can be so beautiful.'

He rubbed his eyes, opened them, shut them, opened them again, and smiled. Suddenly he flung his arms round me.

'Son of my noble past,' he exclaimed, 'shall we start a new life? Shall we fry a dozen eggs, fetch a loaf from the cupboard, knock the top off a bottle of wine? Shall we, in short, begin to live like real human beings?'

I saw that he was still marvellously drunk. His voice had the organ tones of a bright Sunday morning the innocence of a day that has not yet begun.

'Something happened last night,' I said firmly. 'What was it?'

He groped about under the sofa, upset something, and ended by producing a bottle and handing it to me. I broke off the top on the windowsill and poured out the wine.

The huge man drank, remote from the world.

With closed eyes he savoured the wine with every fibre of his body. He was one great mouth and tongue, and then for a brief moment he came back to himself and said in a loud voice:

'Go to the cemetery. Go to the cemetery.'

So I went to the cemetery, and looked at the graves, the gravestones and the brown sandstone war memorial with the names inscribed on it, but discovered nothing, and I was just about to leave when I stopped and went back. Then I discovered that someone had chalked up all our names on the back of the memorial.

I went up close and spelled out the names, my own and the names of all the others, and now I remembered that someone had had the idea. Why not? Which one of us had not been killed in action, which of us was not in some way or other buried, wounded, forgotten?

A fine rain was falling, and at the foot of the memorial there was a bit of chalk. I picked it up. Before the rain washed them away I wanted for the sake of justice to add all the names that should be added. Heaven knows how long I went on writing. When you start thinking about them, you remember more names than you can write down.

Then, when I left the village and hurried off to catch the train, I felt much better. I held out my ticket to the ticket collector and said:

'These living persons are a strange race of dead.'

'I beg your pardon?' the man said in surprise.

'I only meant the supplement,' I said hurriedly. 'I'll pay it in the train.'

INSCRIPTIONS

ALL that was over and done with. It belonged to the past.

He walked hesitantly, irresolutely along the row of workmen, leaning back as if he were reluctant to follow his feet and wanted to turn back, or wished he had done so already. The workmen took no notice of him, but went on sullenly working away with hammer and chisel, causing precise shapes to appear in the stone under their hands and tools and rousing a fine, thin mist of stone-dust.

'Hi, where do you come from?' one of them called out. The eyes in his emaciated face were red-rimmed.

'From the valley,' the new arrival replied.

'You won't regret it,' the man said, and spat, and went on with his hammering. 'You won't regret it,' he repeated.

None of the others troubled about him, because they were busy, and the foreman came and handed him his tools and showed him where he was to work, and so he soon forgot this scrap of conversation and what it might have meant.

He asked what he was to carve on the stone, and the foreman produced a piece of paper and showed him the pattern to follow, and he took his hammer and chisel and set to work.

At first he kept casting regretful glances in the direction of the valley, but soon he was caught up in the rhythm and he felt as if a secret piece of music were being played or a message communicated to him, and he went on hammering away, and eventually saw that his bit of stone was carved precisely like the pattern on the piece of paper, he examined it minutely and saw they corresponded in every detail, and he called over the foreman, whose practised eye at once saw when work had been done properly. 'Well done, you've made a good job of it,' he said, and collected the tools.

They nodded to each other. 'Have a rest,' the gentle foreman said. The newcomer was tired, he felt he had been working, he was tired, tired to death, and he dropped to the ground and lay on his back, with his feet towards the stone. He lay there with his hands folded on his stomach, looking at his handiwork and feeling pleased with it, with the world and with himself.

When he realised it was his own name he had carved into the stone it was too late.

The world is covered with cemeteries. Stone messages announcing innumerable last days. All that is over and done with. All that will be over and done with.

CREATION

Go on. Keep hurrying on. Go on breathing, singing, swearing, copulating, telling lies, keeping your mouth shut. You are still the whole desolate race in a single person. You are still the ocean with a gale blowing force twelve, and you are still the ship on it. You are still sinking. You are on fire. You are the rusty wrecks under the mud, and you are the mute fish. You are flesh and bone. You are our children. You are our gods. Pray to us. Reject us. Make us ever new. Go on killing us. Make us ever different. Make us pain and big clouds. Make us mountains and seas. Make us white faces with round eyes and open mouths. Make us dreams. Make us heavy black dreams under the bed. Make us light, gold-spun dreams under the bed. Make us light as feathers. Make us as heavy as stone. You are feathers. You are stone. You are stone. You are feathers. You are wind. You have been. You have never been. You have ceased to exist. You have never ceased to exist. You are alive and dead and buried and putrefied. You.

I turn myself into a flag
pull it down
farewell, this is death,
only putrefication remains.

I put myself at half-mast,
I mourn myself for five minutes.
Not long or a great deal. Just a quick visit,
worms gnaw bones fallow.

All the same it was worth it.
One cried a little, lived from day to day,

Lived sometimes here and sometimes there.
There was no more in it than that.

Of course fir woods and children
remain behind.
Also governments, several dozen of them,
and slaughterhouse-red cattle.

Oh, now I'm a daisy
plucked quite small
in nobody's honour.

Let us live. Let us want. Let us want this and
that and that and this. We too want to kill Jews.
We awake and are Jews. We awake and are killed.
We awake and beg for mercy. We awake lying in
front of ourselves. We awake and look at ourselves
pitilessly. We awake and see our knives sunk into
our bodies. We awake and pray. We awake and
bleed. We awake and do not awake. We awake and
awake no more. We awake and are Jews. We awake
and are murderers. We awake and see ourselves.
We awake and are. We awake and have been.

We are and have been. Now go. Now go as a
messenger and bleed your own pain into the sand
instead of mine. Now go and say

And say what vulture-clawed
Marxism is about.
You feel it inside you
drag on your nameless exile
drag on
You feel it inside you
vulture-clawed exile
and vulture-clawed temptation

and vulture-clawed solitude
and vulture-clawed pain
pain?
cast behind you your pain of yesterday
prepare
for today's
cast behind you today's pain
prepare
for tomorrow's

hold your face up to the wind
expose your memory to despair
doubt your own honesty
test the permanence of your grief
fight unrest with loyalty
loyalty with unrest
you – oh, you
me – oh, me
in the hollow of my mask
my face assumes a suitable expression
towards you

My ancient enemy,
and everyone conceals
your name.

I want a gentle world. I want a marvellously
strange world. I want a world like a huge bed and a
huge bottle of wine and an inexhaustible maternal
bosom. I want sisters with kind faces and brothers
with eyes like black coals. I want words fit to be
carved in stone and a good, round, full silence. I
want a fatherland for no hostile purpose. I want a
fatherland that would be like a father and a real

father with a lot of friendly brothers. I want un-betrayed mothers. I want gentle people. I want people with few wishes for themselves and many for others. I want good human beings. I want beautiful human beings. I want human beings. I want human beings. Human wishes. Human wishes are worthy wishes. I want human beings of worth. I want worth for human beings.

Raise your hand till it is black. Keep your eye open till it falls out. Give your words weight till they smash the floors in. Make yourself as irresis-tible as a shell out of a gun. Make yourself as big as a cathedral. Make yourself as black as night, as hot as the sun, as cold as the moon, as silent as the grave, as eloquent as a newspaper. Make youself clever. Make yourself stupid. Make yourself ill. Make yourself intolerable. Make yourself agreeable. Make yourself strong. Make yourself weak. Make yourself a Negro. Make yourself a Jew. Sacrifice yourself. Make yourself a murderer. Make your-self an avenger. Make yourself a fugitive. Make yourself hard. Make yourself soft. Make yourself human. Make yourself animal. Make yourself God.

The realm of dreams is the realm
of freedom.